OUT OF THE BASEMENT

A Novel

By James Rourke

Published 2020

Printed in the United States of America
Print ISBN: 978-1-951490-42-3
E-book ISBN: 978-1-951490-43-0

Publisher Information:
DartFrog Books
4697 Main Street
Manchester Center, VT 05255

www.DartFrogBooks.com

PERMISSIONS

For Juliana, Logan, Alice,
Rayden, and Jo-Jo

Chase your dreams, loved ones.
Chase your dreams.

ACKNOWLEDGEMENT

The completion of a manuscript is a solo job. A manuscript becoming a book requires a team effort and I am so pleased to spend some time thanking those who helped me along the way.

Rebecca Holdridge, Karen Diaz, Lorraine Dooley, Lauren Girasoli, and Brian Girasoli were the first readers and their collective feedback helped shape the early rounds of editing. Patrick Kirker invested a great deal of time discussing the book and the power of music. Each conversation brought new insights into the creative process. Heather Doughty, owner of HBD Edits, provided a professional eye, an open ear, and thoughtful suggestion over three rounds of editing. I would not be at this point without Heather.

Thanks to Gordon McClellan founder of DartFrog Books for his vision and the opportunity I've been granted. Members of the DartFrog team that have assisted me include Ali Trowbridge, Carrie Gessner, Suanne Laqueur, and Marina Aris.

Finally, this book is dedicated to my four children and my grandson. This book is about a man chasing a dream while terrified by the prospects of doing so. I'm fairly certain that fear is part of the process of growth and I sincerely hope my children and grandson always find a way to overcome one in pursuit of the other. Honestly, I hope all people do, for the more energized and fearless dreamers there are in the world the better off the world will be.

SUGGESTED LISTENING

Chapter 24: Bruce Springsteen, "Thunder Road" *Born to Run*
Bruce Springsteen, "Tougher than the Rest" *Tunnel of Love*
Chapter 25: Bruce Springsteen, "Bobby Jean" *Born in the U.S.A.*
Chapter 26: Bruce Springsteen, "Real World" *Human Touch*
Bruce Springsteen, "No Surrender" *Born in the U.S.A.*
Bruce Springsteen, "Born to Run" *Born to Run*

Once thoroughly broken down,
who is he that can repair the damage?
-Frederick Douglass, *My Bondage and My Freedom*

CHAPTER 1
A MEDITATION ON PAIN

We have all been told that if we search the primordial darkness, we will find our precious light. The diamond deep in the earth awaits discovery by the weary traveler. Such a cherished fantasy, an idea steeped in delusion—the preferred mindset of idealistic dreamers. There are no diamonds in the secret places of the earth; there is only the darkness of the pit.

Foolishly, I still crawl through this cavern. Do I somehow cling to the fable of the light? I am more fool than prophet, crawling because I am too dimwitted to stop. I chew dirt, one mouthful upon another. My teeth shatter on stone. My nails peel from my fingers, a sacrifice to the unforgiving rock. Fool am I as I continue to search for diamonds, having been told by men I call wise that they are hidden in this darkness. Gems are not mine to have. Maggots and lice are the reward of my faith. The holes I dig open not to treasure but to the abyss. The treacherous precipice calls me, a sweet release from my labors. My death would not matter. Clumsily, I resist the Sirens' call.

Waves of dizziness overwhelm me, causing me to stumble forward.

I do not plummet, but still I fall. Sliding along the jagged stone, my skin is ripped and shredded. I am flayed by my efforts to rebuke the void. Tumbling uncontrolled, I crash onto a slab of rock, filthy and unforgiving. Blood mixes with the muck. I know instantly that my life's fluid will not regenerate the barren waste. This is no blood rite; it is a bloodletting. Nothing else. These wounds will not heal. Scars will run along my body like fault lines in the Earth. As those mighty fissures shake the planet to its core, so my marks will rend my very soul. Do I even have one? Was it lost long ago in the sub-terranean dark? Did I ever possess such a thing? Could it have been shattered by a mighty quake, leaving me a husk, an incomplete man? I would pray for answers, but I believe I have lost that right.

Still I rise. Again. Always. What stubbornness is this? Too witless to realize hope is dead, I stand on wobbly legs. I do not know why I choose to amble forward, ever deeper into the darkness, into the pit. The shadows, however, are not impenetrable. As I stagger, my eyes unexpectedly develop unnatural nocturnal vision. I am gifted with the ability to see an arm's length ahead. Is this some form of mockery? Am I not encountering bleakness that cannot be dis-pelled? Why am I taunted with this limited sight now?

A low growl echoes in the unbounded cave. A snarl from ev-erywhere and, thus, nowhere. Oh my god, is he here? Hunting? Searching? I do not feel his presence, his horror in this dark place. Is he merely in my thoughts? Forever haunting. I don't know—I can't. No more. I am not safe here, anxious and bleeding, but I am alone. Without a path I persist. Groping. Lurching. Graceless. I have reached it, but it's not the dragon's treasure or the lone diamond in the yawn-ing hollow. I have not found a blossom in the muck or reached some distant and beautiful shore. No, I have found you. The Door. My Door.

Why am I before you again? Has this not been settled? Did

Pandora not teach us well enough? Some portals, like the Box of Set, should remain unopened. Yet the Door taunts me. Summons me, after all this time, to find it here in the darkness. Still here. Always here. Daring me to enter, knowing I am a coward feigning courage.

I run my hands along your rough wooden engravings. I feel images that make little sense to me; the gibberish of lunatics engraved in wood. Confusion reigns where understanding is sought. I feel your arch, carved and ornate. My fingers, bleeding and gnarled, find a doorplate with no name. Lastly, my hands come upon your knocker. Such a useless thing, for I know knocking alone never permits passage. Only my own courage and strength will grant me entrance. My strength. What folly. Would that I were Arthur before Excalibur or Thor with his magic gloves, ready to hoist Mjolnir and strike down my foes. I am not such a man. There is no mythic strength coursing in my veins. No gods are with me. I am small. I have been called, again, to a place of defeat and humiliation. Why have I been called back? Why do I answer? I possess enough strength to suppress the desire to weep before you. On my knees, struggling not to drown in another torrent of meaningless tears. At least I can claim that shallow victory. Enough tears have been shed here. I should not have come back.

CHAPTER 2
MORNING MEETING

Michael Tanner shot up in bed and gasped. Panting in a preconscious delirium, his hands searched for wounds. *Holy fuck.* As he ensured his fingernails were in place—*so fuckin' real*—his tongue rubbed his teeth. Satisfied that the wounds from his nightmare did not carry into his waking hours, he began scanning the room. The remnants of his nightmare and the starless early morning sky brought strange images to his addled mind. For a moment, the mythic Door of his dream state appeared before him, only to fade into the bathroom door. The floor of the rocky cavern flattened out into brown wall-to-wall carpeting. Michael rubbed his forehead as normal breathing resumed.

"Fuck. Fuck. Fuck," Michael mumbled to the empty room. He inhaled, deliberately and controlled, holding the breath for an extended period before peacefully exhaling. Concerned the ground was an illusion, Michael gently probed the floor with his feet. Satisfied with the carpet's safety, he carefully rose on still-shaking legs. "Okay. Okay." He settled into himself. "Holy fuck."

Michael surveyed the room, a final reassurance that his surroundings were indeed merely a hotel room, and groaned a final,

"Fuck." It had been three weeks now; three grueling weeks in which sleeping more than four hours on any given night was a blessing. He wished he could blame it on the stress of the tumultuous publicity tour for his new book, *Bruce and Buddha: How Rock and Roll and Ancient Wisdom can be your Guide*. Written more for personal pleasure than commercial concerns, the book was an unexpected hit. The four-week-old promotional tour happened to coincide with his recent sleeplessness. It was this fact alone that led his agent, Brian Murphy, and the publicist, Melissa Burns, assigned to the author by Idea Publishing, to conclude the tour was the culprit.

Michael knew better. He suspected as much early in this latest bout of sleeplessness. His recent meditations only confirmed that something else was festering within him. Something else robbed him of sleep and darkened his thoughts. *Fuck it. Worry about that shit later.* At forty-five years old, Michael had become quite comfortable with certain aspects of himself. One thing he knew, he always allowed himself space for reflection. It could be in the shower. It could be during a walk. It could be in the middle of a hallway with people walking by and wondering if he had slipped into some kind of trance. No need to force it. And sure as hell no need to start the wheel turning now because it was 4:30 in the morning. *Try to get some more sleep.* Michael laughed, realizing he likely had a better chance of completing a marathon than sleeping, for despite his protests, his mind raced over the images of his latest nightmare.

Michael picked up his cell phone and pulled up the name Sara Torrey, Brian's assistant. Perhaps he should message her. The two worked well together, and she was increasingly a source of comfort to him. He paused and put down the phone. No need to text her at this hour. It just would not be professional. Michael sought out the bottle of whiskey that helped him fall asleep three hours earlier. He poured a glass over ice, hoping lightning would strike twice.

Settling into a plush chair, he sipped on his drink and began writing in his journal, which lay on the small table situated on the chair's left arm. The pen and the drink did their collective jobs of calming Michael, allowing him to fall asleep a mere half-hour before his cell phone's alarm brought him back to the world.

The shrill beeping jarred him to consciousness. He turned off the effective, if unwanted, sound and saw it was 7:00. *The morning meeting. Get focused.* In an attempt to shake off the latest round of morning cobwebs, Michael placed both hands over his face and slowly pulled them down off his chin. *Okay. Get ready. Game face.* Michael knew he had time for a shower and a shave. Well, definitely a shower. The shave could be decided by a coin flip. What was not negotiable was the need for coffee. Coffee would be a most welcome friend.

Thirty-seven minutes later, Michael was out of the shower and dressed in blue jeans and a black T-shirt. He rubbed a towel over his graying hair and hesitantly reached for a brush. Evaluating himself in the mirror, he ignored the brush and merely ran his hands through his hair, pulled it in a couple of directions, and found himself satisfied with the almost controlled mess atop his head. As a brush never fixed his hair, a razor did not shave his face. Coffee had also yet to touch his lips. Checking his cell, he smiled. Plenty of time to get to the hotel's breakfast stand, grab a coffee, and go to suite 517 for his meeting.

All went well, and Michael entered the suite at 8:55. He was barely three strides into the room before he heard Sara's voice.

"Morning, Michael." Her greeting was more programmed than personal because her head was down, her focus on her cell phone's notebook. When her eyes turned upwards, shock overwhelmed her friendlier instincts. "Michael? You look awful!"

"Well, thank you, Sara. Good morning to you, too. And may I say, you look lovely."

"Oh, I didn't mean…" Sara attempted to backpedal but, true to her way, quickly doubled down. "You just look awful. Tired! Awfully tired! Did you sleep last night?"

"I get it," Michael acknowledged, raising his coffee cup like he was making a toast. "I may have gotten in a good four hours of sleep last night. I just get a little amped up after those presentations and find it a little difficult to come down. That's all."

"That could be true," Sara's tone became more professional as she calculated the road ahead, "but we have six more weeks on this tour and a possible meeting with Icon Media in three weeks. You need to get some rest."

"Yes, dear," Michael gave a wry smirk. Where the mocking of his target ended and the affection began was difficult to discern. What was clear, however, was his desire to continue to banter rather than turn to business matters.

Sara was poised to respond, but Melissa Burns entered the suite's living quarters to officially begin the meeting.

"Alright, people," Melissa started, her voice sounding like she was still on the phone with the executives. "We have a big day. Holy shit! Mike, what the hell? Did you sleep outside? Where are your shoes?"

"My shoes? That's your big worry? I know we have two photo shoots with national magazines today, the accompanying interviews, and some afternoon talk show. But we don't have to leave the hotel until…." Michael's eyes groped the ceiling, searching for the correct information.

"Eleven," a young man seated on a sofa offered with confidence.

"Eleven. Thank you, Mark," Michael raised his coffee to salute the twenty-five-year-old intern. The devil guided his grin as he repeated, "Eleven. It's 9:13, Melissa. My room, which contains my shoes, is three doors down. Trust me. I got this."

"Fine." Melissa hated this aspect of Michael's personality. She also knew she should do little to encourage it. "Just make sure you let the makeup people touch you up a little bit at the shoot."

"Worried about your brand?"

"You should be worried about your brand," Melissa shot back.

"I worry about the words," Michael responded. "I believe that's what got us here." *I also wonder if the stick up your ass goes all the way up and scrapes the top of your skull or if it stops somewhere in your throat.*

"Alright, everybody. Let's play nice and get on the same page." The words came from Brian Murphy, Michael's agent for fifteen years. His hand fell on Michael's shoulder as he spoke. "We do have a big day and having it all go well is our top priority."

"Of course, Brian," Michael said. "So, what have we got for the itinerary today?"

Brian looked at Melissa, who gestured for him to answer. "To be fair, Melissa has got us on a nice schedule today. Um, you and I will be leaving the hotel at eleven. Head over for the photo shoots downtown. Then the interviews. Sara will meet us at the television studio and make sure everything is in order for your spot there. Meanwhile, Melissa and Mark will be at the evening venue. Half-hour book signing followed by your presentation to one hundred and twenty-five paying customers willing to hear you babble for ninety minutes."

"Ten of the audience members," Melissa interjected while Brian took a seat at a small breakfast table, "will be attending the weekend writing and reflection retreat you are hosting at the end of this tour. You will meet with them after the rest of the audience departs."

"And I will know them by…?" Michael asked.

"I have the details on that," Sara said. "I will make sure the meet and greet runs smoothly."

"If you're in charge, I have no worries at all." Michael communicated his trust in Sara with a warm smile.

Sara allowed a quick tilt of her head in response before continuing, her gaze more focused on Melissa than anyone. "I will also receive confirmation regarding our requests for that weekend event and continue streamlining the schedule. I'll have an update for everyone tomorrow."

Melissa was busy placing a note in her phone. "Excellent."

"Wow," Michael remarked. "Busy day. I should have gotten more sleep. At the very least I should have some shoes. I think I'll go check on them."

Sara, who had been with Brian for seven years and had been working with Michael for a year and a half, was now accustomed to Michael's mannerisms and personality. Whereas a year ago she still had trouble reading him, she now smirked at the comment. She was all the more pleased to see the way he annoyed Melissa. Michael walked by and noticed her smile. He gave her a quick wink and reached for the door handle. "See you in thirty, Brian," Michael called, entering the hallway.

"Be good," Brian said, waving goodbye.

The dynamic of the group had been strange for about a week. The core group of Michael, Brian, and Sara had been more or less on the road together for the duration of the tour. Brian's relationship with Michael had evolved over the years from the merely professional to, at the least, caring coworkers and occasional confidants. Their work together had achieved limited success but a loyal readership. Brian's unwavering dedication to Michael's work made a profound impression, for Michael was far from the most lucrative client in the stable. This never prevented him from feeling like the most important. Brian's level of dedication led to the opening of windows into their personal lives, like discussing the joys and frustrations of fatherhood. When *Bruce and Buddha: How Rock and Roll and Ancient Wisdom can be your Guide* became an unexpected hit, Brian's professional savvy truly came to bear. He became instrumental in smoothing the sometimes rough waters that would emerge between Michael and the business end of the writing world.

Melissa and Mark attended the kickoff event and then reconnected with the tour five days ago. Mark was a mere two months into his internship. He was content learning the ropes and, unless reminding people of schedules or some other precise note, silently observing. Melissa was a highly efficient professional with a meticulous eye and a penchant for planning every last detail. She was, in some ways, the perfect person to help maintain the momentum being generated by the successful tour. Unfortunately, Michael found her obsessive to the point of oppressive. Not that he did not appreciate the importance of deadlines; he just arrived at them in a manner that was an irritant to type A personalities. His disinterest in exact details and tendency to ignore the minutia that obviously concerned Melissa put the two almost constantly at odds.

"You know he'll be at every event and knock them all out of the park," Brian addressed Melissa, who was offended by Michael's abrupt exit.

"I know. Doesn't mean I like his attitude."

"He knows you don't. That's why he does it."

"That's mature." Melissa scoffed, taking a seat at the table with Brian.

"It ain't about maturity." Brian said. "It's about absurdity."

"You've said that before. I still don't get—"

"I know you don't, but I think we should—"

"You should not encourage him. In fact, he should still be here."

"Do you really want him here? Do you think that will help you?" Brian stood up. "I'll get him. Or do you want to fine-tune our schedule for the next couple days and trust me to handle him?"

"Schedule," Melissa said quickly, "definitely the schedule."

"You're sure?" Brian teased, stepping toward the door. "I can go get him. Not a problem."

"No," a now smiling Melissa confirmed. "I think we're fine."

"Alright then," Brian returned to his seat at the small table. Sara, who all but ignored Brian's exchange with Melissa, took a seat on a couch and looked at her notes. After ten seconds, she paced the room, sat on a counter, and eventually returned to the more comfortable couch. Brian thought nothing of the constant movement while Melissa continued her inner struggle to accept Sara's roaming.

The discussion began. It was not long before Sara was interjecting. She didn't say much but was always spot on in her assessment of timing events or troubleshooting venues. Brian wondered, as he had for a number of months, how much longer he could keep her on his payroll. Mark watched and listened, knowing any questions he had regarding the process he witnessed would be answered at some point. It took Melissa twenty-seven minutes to reach a sense of satisfaction that everyone's duties for the day were clarified. The count included necessary double-checking, which felt more punitive than productive to Sara.

Brian leaned back and cracked his neck. "Alright. I am going to help Michael find his shoes. See you at the studio, Sara. Melissa and Mark, I will catch up with you at the hotel convention center later tonight. All good?"

"All good," Sara confirmed. She gathered her belongings to head to her next task.

"Very good, indeed," Melissa concurred, the team's efficiency helped erase her annoyance at Michael.

CHAPTER 3
A WRITER'S VISION

Michael groaned as he sat up in bed. He guessed it was 2:30 a.m. He was nearly correct as a quick glance at his cell phone revealed it was 2:43. While slightly off on the time, there were two other things he felt very sure of. The first; the ceiling he had been staring at for the past twenty minutes was not terribly interesting. The second; sleep was not in his immediate future. What to do? The bottle of whiskey on the nightstand did not seem inviting and his journal was not calling his name. An unusual urge hit and he chuckled as he progressed to the dresser. Pulling open the top drawer revealed his copy of *Bruce and Buddha: How Rock and Roll and Ancient Wisdom can be your Guide*. Book in hand, he returned to bed and switched on the nightlight.

The Prologue to *Bruce and Buddha: How Rock and Roll and Ancient Wisdom can be your Guide*
"Prologue: Greetings from..."

Hello, dear reader, and greetings from, well, not Asbury Park. At this point in time, I am writing to you from the computer in my home office. I am honored, truly honored, that you are reading these words. You see, when you're alone at your computer, you don't know if a manuscript will ever become a book. If it should become a book, will it find readers? The fact that it has is immensely gratifying. I hope the time I have invested into sculpting these chapters is worthy of the time you will spend reading them. I hope the constructed lessons and heartfelt messages find open hearts and receptive minds. So begins the unusual relationship between writer and reader, a faceless meeting of strangers sustained by the power and mystery of ideas. In some ways, it connects me to the two great sages who are the foundation of this journey.

Some twenty-five hundred years ago, Siddhartha Gautama left his royal life on a search to find the path that would lead to the end of suffering. He joined various religious communities and for seven years, lived with wise men. In time, however, each teacher he sought exhausted their lessons, leaving the young seeker disenchanted and answerless. Siddhartha, utilizing the accumulated knowledge from his quest, decided to meditate on the problem of suffering. In the profound silence between heartbeats, he found an answer to his query and became the Buddha. Soon thereafter, he delivered his first sermon to five monks at the deer park in Sarnath, India—not far from where the flow of the Varuna River becomes one with the life-giving Ganges. Thus Buddhism was introduced to the world, promulgating powerful lessons for over two millennia. Sarnath became one of its holy sites.

Some fifty years ago, a guitar-slinging, raspy voiced, scruffy, and determined twenty-four-year-old Bruce Springsteen earned the opportunity to introduce himself to the world. It was the product of a different form of discipline, but Springsteen––much like Siddhartha–carved his own path with singular determination. Where Siddhartha left his familial home, Bruce's family left him. At the age of twenty, he chose to stay in the holy land of Freehold, New Jersey. But even before this parting of ways, Bruce was studying at the feet of his own spiritual masters: Sinatra, Presley, and the Beatles. He honed his craft by working in isolation on his melodic meditations, seeking truths found only in a soul awakened by music. Through a journey of local bands and numberless low paying gigs, Bruce fought, scraped, and built a reputation. His conviction led to his first sermon, delivered on the album Greetings from Asbury Park, N.J. and The Stone Pony became a holy site.

"Koi paraga?" was the rallying cry of the Buddha. Translated to English, "Anyone for the other shore?" The other shore is located across a dark and formidable sea. Most fear to even attempt the journey, comfortable with the familiar sand beneath their feet and, by extension, comfortable with the suffering they think is unavoidable. Others climb into rafts, a commonly used metaphor in Buddhism, and seek the other shore. Fear, however, grips their hearts when they move into uncharted waters. An abyss seems to open before them, and they return to their homeland. The battle cry in the form of a question is heard again, "Koi paraga?" That it is a question is most fitting, for you get to choose. Will you dare the abyss and seek the other shore where you can be freed from the diseased mind and pathological thoughts that bring suffering? Can you face the fear of the vast unknown, trusting yourself to ferry your raft to a shore where compassion will fill your very being and infuse your relationships with uncommon depth? You may become something greater than you have ever been, even though you may well appear undistinguished. You, too, can be a gift to the world if you can traverse this hostile sea. Grab your raft and face your fears. There are great rewards for those who complete the journey.

"Anyone alive out there?" The first time I heard Bruce Springsteen raise his battle cry question was in Boston during his reunion tour. He was a man in command of his message and had the full power of the legendary E Street Band behind him. I heard the question and cried out, "Yes," even though somewhere deep inside I wasn't so sure. I wanted to be alive. I wanted to feel that energy coming from a source inside myself and not an external one. "Anyone alive out there?" The call came again, and I roared my praise, knowing full well what I truly needed to do was accept the challenge to face my own inner storms. Bruce never asked anyone to get on a raft and face the waters of doubt, but he surely asked us to get into cars and face the journey of our lives. From earlier albums, we were encouraged to claim the highway and live the adventure of "Born to Run" or escape the mundane by navigating the path laid out in "Thunder Road." As Bruce progressed in life and songwriting, he implored us to find the "Land of Hope and Dreams" and dared us to care enough to live by the mantra "We Take Care of our Own." Get on your raft or into your car. Face the fear. Feel the pain and dream anyway. Live! Live for yourself and others.

Both Bruce and Buddha cut through the false dichotomy of individual or community concerns. There are enough hours in our days, years, and in our lives to do both. Buddhism, like most schools of thought, splits into competing schools. Theravada Buddhism, the way of the elders, unapologetically promotes the necessity to take responsibility for our own growth by becoming an ever-increasing best version of ourselves so we become better equipped to aid others. The ideal individual in Theravada Buddhism is the arhat, the wandering dedicated disciple. Wisdom is the arhat's primary virtue. The pursuit and attainment of wisdom allows for profound insight into the nature of reality and the fundamental causes of human anxiety.

Another school is Mahayana Buddhism, the great raft or vehicle. The ideal individual in this school is the bodhisattva, who chooses to be reborn again and again. A bodhisattva stays in the world despite gaining liberation from the cycle of reincarnation. The reason the bodhisattva chooses containment is simplicity in itself: to be of assistance to others. Compassion is their primary virtue, even more important than wisdom. Its cultivation is essential. Wisdom, to be clear, is important, but it takes years to cultivate. Compassionate action can be taken today, so live it now.

Bruce Springsteen has not divided himself into competing schools of music, but his immense song catalog illuminates twin goals of individual and communal growth. Through the course of this book, we see Bruce exhibit traits of both the arhat and the bodhisattva, even though the embodiment of these ideals was never his goal. Truth, however, rises in our lives without our consent, and I hope Mr. Springsteen forgives me for what I intend to be a most respectful use of his art and biography to help us find our way to a better way of living. Perhaps he can help us find something even greater than that. Rest assured, our glory days are not yet behind us.

I have no great initial sermon from a park or a vehicle to usher you into. What I can say is this: I heard the call to the other shore and the request to live. I was afraid of the raft and can't claim to have lived my life to the fullest. But the summons has been heard, and the only way I knew to answer was through my thoughts that became words. The words became this book. This book has laid out a vision that has helped me find my courage. My quest for ideas and the right words served me, and I hope they steer you in a positive direction as well. In the end, I think a teacher must have the will to live his most *important words and the ability to deliver at least one powerful lesson that maybe, just maybe, enriches the soul of the student. This book is that lesson, but only you can tell me if it succeeds. Wouldn't it be nice to find each other on the other shore even though we have never met? I would say that sounds like a bit much to ask from a book, but Bruce and Buddha taught me to dream, and I would hate to let them down.*

Mythology is not a lie, mythology is poetry, it is metaphorical.
It has been well said that mythology is the penultimate truth—
penultimate because the ultimate cannot be put into words.
It is beyond words. Beyond images, beyond that bounding rim
of the Buddhist Wheel of Becoming. Mythology pitches the
mind beyond that rim, to what can be known but not told.
-Joseph Campbell, *The Power of Myth*

CHAPTER 4

HOW DID WE GET HERE?

"Alright!" Brian clapped his hands twice and guided Michael into a corridor that led away from the blinding photo studio. "Photo shoot is over. Interview is set to begin."

"Damn, Brian," Michael teased, slightly shocked, "you're a little extra pumped up today. You're even walking fast."

"What can I say? While these promos are, as you know, good for building the success of *Bruce and Buddha*, they are also good for your other works. All this publicity has got my phone buzzing the past three days regarding some of your lesser known works."

The duo stepped onto an elevator. "That's great! You always said that's what would happen."

"That I did," Brian boasted, visibly pleased with the unfolding events. The elevator doors slid open, and Brian prepared to bound into the next leg of their trip. He stopped, however, when he felt Michael's palm on his chest, pressuring him to stay on the elevator.

Michael hit the "close door" button, and the doors slid shut. He looked at the ceiling, weighing the words that fought to be uttered. Settling on the simplest expression, he looked directly at his agent. "I just wanted to, well, say thank you, Brian." Michael sighed, briefly rubbing his forehead before a placid smile settled onto his face. "I don't even know how we got here. I mean, my work went nowhere for years, and you never quit on me. I appreciate that. I really do. You've been very good to me."

"Hey, no problem. Fighting the fight is what we do, right? I always told you I liked your writing, and all we had to do was find the right publisher and things would move. You write with a real purpose, and people are starting to see it. Give yourself some credit, too." Brian paused before adding a final thought. "And, yes, I know that's hard for you."

Michael grabbed Brian's shoulder and laughed. "You know I hate appreciation tennis. Just because I said something nice about you doesn't mean you have to send it back." *I don't deserve these accolades.*

"Understood. You ready to go? Or are we going to share some more?"

"I think the moment is gone. Why don't you hit the 'open door' button before I regret being kind to you."

"That's more like it," Brian teased, following Michael's instruction. The two men stepped into the hallway. After four strides, Brian gave in to the desire to resume needling his author. "I gotta say, you made me nervous. The way you stopped me from getting off the elevator—the whole hand on my chest thing. I was afraid you were going to proposition me or something."

"Sorry to let you down, boss," Michael deadpanned as they proceeded down the corridor. "Maybe some other time."

Two quick turns and Michael found himself in a comfortable sitting room. A woman about his age sat in a plush chair in front of a sofa. A pen and paper resided on a coffee table to her left. Brian, realizing she did not notice them enter because she was fiddling with a digital voice recorder, gently announced their arrival. "Hello, Mrs. Holland. Are we early?"

"Oh!" she exclaimed, sitting up with a start. "Sorry, no. You're fine. I was just checking my recorder for the fifteenth time. Just my own little version of OCD. Please, call me Wendy."

"Hello, Wendy. I'm Brian, and this is Michael Tanner."

Michael extended his hand. "Nice to meet you, Wendy. We all have a little OCD. I can't leave the house without triple-checking if all the lights are off."

"Is that OCD, or just the fact you're a father?" Wendy good-naturedly inquired.

Michael overemphasized a contemplative look. "I think one might lead to the other."

"Very true," Wendy conceded. "Would you like something, maybe a bottled water before we get started? Or a soda?"

"A water would be nice."

Wendy turned to send an intern for bottled water, but Brian interrupted. "No need to get the help. I got it. Not much else for me to do now that I've successfully delivered Michael to you."

"That's not necessary," responded Wendy. Brian shook her off and exited the room. Whether or not he appreciated the irony that he had to ask an intern for guidance to the floor's small pantry remained a mystery.

"He's not always that nice," Michael noted. "I just gave him a compliment in the hall, and now he's sucking up to me."

Wendy laughed for a moment. "Nice to have good people around you."

"Yes, it is," Michael agreed. He allowed his mind to wander to thoughts of friends and his daughters, whose support was essential. His attention returning to the room, he looked quizzically at Wendy. "Did you just start the interview?"

"Well," Wendy confessed, her finger turning on the recorder, "while I would like to discuss various chapters, including the one about relationships, I thought we would start with the concept itself. The book, at times, sounds so simple, and yet I felt I was learning a lot about an array of topics and disciplines. The ideas seemed quite divergent, but you tied everything together. How did you do that?"

"I guess because I started with a very basic premise," Michael began, his eyes moving from Wendy to the window behind her. He stared out the window peacefully for no more than a second before his gaze turned back to the interviewer. "That premise being that, in the end, I'm a simple guy."

"Aristotle, Buddha, Abraham Maslow, Bruce Springsteen, and Metallica woven together, somehow, with the *Lord of the Rings* and 1984 to make a perfectly clear argument about the necessity of building personal integrity, of seeking and maintaining healthy relationships, the need to maintain hope while struggling through difficult times, and you provide tips on how to apply these lessons to your life. All of that takes place, and you want me to believe this starts from a place of simplicity? You'll have to do better than that. So I ask again, how did you weave all these ideas together?"

Wendy's question hung in the air while Michael moved forward on the sofa. His feet were now planted solidly on the ground, and his elbows were resting on his knees. Michael's head dropped until it was low enough that he could have held it in his hands but did not. They were some six inches from his head, fingers spread as if emitting energy. His green eyes looked up from the floor until they locked on Wendy's. He sat up a little, straightening his back. Words came slowly at first and simmered with a slow burning intensity.

"I am not saying that to be humble; I'm trying to be honest. There are some 4,000 years of reflection—by great and worthy minds—regarding the human condition. I try to understand these thoughts and utilize them as a guide in my own life. So I read. I write. The great sage Confucius once said, paraphrasing here, that he was not a creator but a transmitter. He studied the teachings of the ancients and brought them to China. There are great teachers, you see, and I am not one of them." *Very far from it.* "I can, however, walk in their minds. I can try to learn and transmit their lessons. In particular, I seek those lessons that have the potential to elevate a person and, dare I say, even a community, so people may well enjoy the flourishing life. But I am just a simple man, hoping that my struggles to understand my humanity will be of service to others. That's all." *And much, much less.*

"If I decide to accept that," Wendy carefully watched Michael settle back into the sofa, "then why the forays into music and literature? You touch on modern psychology and even films. Why not just stick with the philosophers? Or just Buddha since he is featured in the title? Stick with one topic?"

Michael smiled broadly, leaning even further into the sofa. He spread his arms along the back cushions and crossed his legs. His eyes glistened slightly as he watched Brian return to the room with two bottles of water. "Hey, Brian," Michael said as he reached for a bottle. "Wendy wants to know why the music and movie references."

"Oh." Brian held a bottle to Wendy. She politely declined. "You see, Michael is an idiot."

"There you have it," Michael stated triumphantly. "Idiocy was the key."

"Idiocy? That's the key?" Wendy's incredulous look added layers of strength to the simple question.

"Well, I suppose it is important to know what is meant by that," Michael confessed as he leaned forward again.

"And what might that be?"

"A professor of psychology, Barry Farber, wrote a book called *Rock 'n' Roll Wisdom*. The basic premise was that insightful songwriters can, sometimes quite unintentionally, succinctly capture the essence of a profound psychological truth or theory. There are many intuitive armchair psychologists among us. Other times, they are intentionally wrestling with meaningful and complex issues. Now, because of their skills and acumen, some people, artists, can help make sense of complex ideas. I find that when puzzled by some philosophical concept, inevitably, I can watch a film or listen to a song, and it helps me make sense of the larger idea. Sometimes the arts are the gateway to understanding. Dare I say the gateway to our very humanity? At least it's that way for me. And the reader is stuck with me as the author."

"Well I suppose the reader could be stuck with a worse author," Wendy teased. "Still, I'm curious: you said that sometimes in a state of confusion you will watch a movie or listen to a song, and it will help make sense of things. Do you seek out certain movies or songs, or is it just haphazard?"

"Well," Michael stretched the word out, allowing it to fill the silence while he sought a helpful explanation. Finding a thought that offered clarity, he continued. "I think that it's quite situational. I can remember in the course of writing my book that Springsteen's "Streets of Fire" was stuck in my head. Just hammering at me. I couldn't listen to it enough to get it out. I was working on a chapter at the time and had to shelve it. In fact, I shelved it permanently, and that chapter was not included in the book at all. I ended up using "Streets of Fire" as the backbone of a much better chapter about—"

"Evaluating the idea of when people are too far gone. What that looks like. What it means to be too far gone."

"Right!" Michael exclaimed passionately. "Maybe I am too far gone, never to return to the light. Maybe, just maybe, I'm too far gone right now for you, but in three years, I emerge with the help of someone else or by my own effort or, in most cases, a combination of the two."

"That was a fascinating chapter. But it wasn't planned?"

"No. I hope this makes sense: it felt demanded of me. But back to your previous question. There are other times when I am perplexed by an idea and just, quite literally, start channel surfing. No rhyme or reason. Just clicking. Sometimes that goes nowhere but other times, damn! I watch for fifteen minutes, and just the scene I need to see is playing before me."

"That's quite a coincidence," Wendy commented.

"Jung would say there are no coincidences. Or at least that some coincidences are meaningful. The mystery of synchronicity."

"Do you subscribe to that?"

"I have friends who do. To be honest with you, I struggle with that idea. It's just a little too poetic for a man like me. It disturbs me because of the temptation to feel that moment of synchronicity and then force meaning into it. It can be difficult to just let things be. To not seek control." Michael's voice trailed off as memories, fears, and hopes suddenly swirled about him. Shaking his head in an attempt to chase ghosts and angels, he quickly continued. "You better watch out. I may start quoting Lao Tzu soon."

"If you feel so inclined, Michael."

"Of course," Michael said, appreciating the encouragement and yet choosing to steer the conversation away from Carl Jung and back to how the popular culture references were woven into his work, "there are also times when an idea is difficult for me to grasp. I, with great intent, reach for a song or film that I know will help me. And they do."

"That's fascinating," Wendy blurted out a bit quicker than intended. "But I would like to return to your aversion."

"My aversion?"

"To synchronicity."

Deep burrows appeared in Michael's forehead, causing his eyes to shrink into small slits. A sip of water allowed his expression and mind to loosen. "Synchronicity? Is this interview about me or my book?"

"I don't see why it can't be about both." Wendy gave a friendly grin, attempting to soften inquisitive eyes.

Michael paused, weighing the implication and possibilities for discovery in Wendy's statement. He smiled and looked at Brian. "How are we doing on time, boss? I get the feeling this might take a while."

Brian checked the clock on his cell. "We're good. We do have other engagements today, Mrs. Holland. I'll let you know if we are close to a necessary departure."

"Excellent," Wendy said. "Seems like we have quite a bit to explore."

"She has no fuckin' idea," Brian whispered to himself as Wendy reengaged Michael with his favorite activity, the exchange of ideas.

We cannot live for ourselves alone. Our lives are connected by a thousand invisible threads, and along these sympathetic fibers our actions run as causes and return to us as results.
-Rev. Henry Melvill, sermon 1855

CHAPTER 5
Q&A

"So, I would like to conclude this presentation with a brief reminder of the key points we covered." Michael stood at center stage in an auditorium holding about three hundred people. He was clearly in a comfortable space, an easy smile and controlled-but-contagious energy emanating from his core. Every eye was trained on him, and it seemed the majority of the audience members carried notepads and pens to capture the author's thoughts. "Who is in your trench? We all need people we know, and I mean KNOW, we can count on when the storms are coming, and the darkness dominates for far too long. We all need reliable foul-weather friends. If you know who yours are, find the time to thank them within the next four weeks. Now please, don't rush off and shoot them a quick text when this event ends. That'll make it, at the least, seem a bit forced. At worst, it'll make it appear you just left some cult meeting and are following the orders of your new guru! That is utterly unacceptable.

"This brings us to our second point: trust the process. By that I mean, you don't have to force certain conversations or interactions into your day. I almost guarantee that, if you just wait on the idea of thanking your foul-weather friend, some very natural moment will arise in the next month, and the conversation can be had within the rhythms of life, not the desperation of one checking off a list.

"And lastly, be aware, dare I say awed, by the interconnected-ness of life. All of us encounter people that could use a little help-ing hand. A little encouragement." Michael was now at the edge of the stage and leaning toward the audience, beseeching them to feel the sincerity of his words. "Sometimes that person is us and by helping the other, we find the energy to keep going ourselves. Then, because we persevere, we encounter other people who had the time or energy to reach out to us. The truly great thing is your life is a testament to what I'm saying. I guarantee at least half the room has had that moment when some person says just the right thing, at just the right time, in just the right way for it to have a tre-mendous impact on your day and disposition. Sometimes it hap-pens when least expected. It wasn't planned, but what you needed found you. Sometimes the source is unexpected: perhaps someone other than your foul-weather friend made time for you, and you're thankful for it. Your path and the paths of others intertwined and provided a little hope. It wasn't dramatic. Movies aren't made of those small victories, but lives are. I sincerely hope I've added a little something to your lives tonight. Be well, do well, and keep fighting the good fight with all thy might."

The audience cheered when Michael wrapped up his presenta-tion. He waved to a group of people who caught his eye before shak-ing hands with some enthusiastic individuals who had walked to the front of the stage. Three security personnel gently guided them back to their seats. Michael smiled at the settling crowd before retreating to a comfortable chair that was situated in the center of the stage. He sat down and addressed the assemblage. The sound of his voice ended the slight din that arose due to the presentation's completion.

"Okay. We have reached the Q&A section of the evening. There are two microphones set up at the end of either aisle. If anyone wants to approach them and ask a question, feel free. I have nothing but time."

Audience members looked around; some seemed embarrassed to speak, while others just didn't want to be first. After about thirty seconds of heads looking around the room, a middle-aged woman approached a mic. "This is probably not a good question, but what's your favorite Springsteen album?"

Michael beamed and chuckled. "Nothing wrong with that question. My favorite album probably depends on my mood from week-to-week and month-to-month. You know what I'm talking about. I will say this, however: for the purposes of my book, the album I used the most was *Darkness on the Edge of Town.* So let's go with that."

The woman returned to her seat and was quickly replaced before the microphone stand by a young man who appeared to be in his mid-twenties. "I was a little confused by something," confessed the new speaker, gripping a writing journal like it was a security blanket. "You mentioned the idea of, um, hold on. I wrote it down. Graceless lurching. The example you used tonight didn't make the idea completely clear to me, but I feel like it's important. Could you, like, try again?"

Michael smirked. "Did you just tell me I didn't do a good job communicating tonight, young man?"

"No! It was great! I just—"

"Whoa! Whoa!" Michael interrupted, holding out both hands. "I was joking, brotha. Relax. Okay, graceless lurching but not the examples from the presentation. Did I mention Simba?"

"Simba?" the confused questioner asked. "From *The Lion King?* Um, no."

"Excellent. All of life's problems can be solved if we turn to *The Lion King.* I am sure it will serve us now. Let me explain, which is what you asked me to do in the first place. You've seen *The Lion King*, right?"

The questioner nodded his head.

"Good." Michael raised his hand like he was about to make a point and suddenly paused. "You know, you don't have to stand there. Could someone get this young man a chair?"

A chair was delivered by a hotel employee, and Michael continued.

"Thanks. Okay. So, you remember the scene where Simba almost gets Nala killed in the elephant graveyard?" A quick nod and Michael continued. "Good. Now you see, Simba was seeking to assert his independence. He was trying to free himself from what he saw to be the constraints placed on him by his father. In doing this, he almost got himself and Nala killed. Now, the Jungian analyst, Kara LaRoux, stresses that when the archetypal energy of the wanderer becomes prevalent in our lives, our first attempts to extend ourselves are often quite awkward. I like the phrase graceless lurching. Sometimes we find ourselves just stumbling around, seeking solid footing and confidence. This helping?"

The young man stood up and spoke into the microphone. "Yeah. It did. Thanks."

"No problem. By the way, could you tell me your name?"

"Uh, Cliff."

"Cliff, do you have something else to ask? You look a little perplexed."

"Well, yeah, actually—but aren't there other people who want to ask you something?"

"I have nothing but time right now," Michael assured his guest, a welcoming smile on his face. "What's up? Let's help each other."

"Well, I'm just not sure how this relates to real life. I get the example you gave, but I'm not seeing how it applies."

"How old are you, Cliff?"

"Twenty-five."

"Perfect." Michael stood. "By this point in your life, either you or a friend has been in a serious relationship that ended. You or your friend could be the breakee or could be the breaker. Doesn't matter. Are you with me, Cliff?"

"Oh yeah," affirmed Cliff, a look of amusement forming on his face while an unshared memory flashed across his mind.

"Interesting," Michael noted, "most people don't look quite so pleased when I bring up the breakee experience. Anyway, the breakee sometimes isn't interested in forming new relationships or avoids personal connections. Sometimes the breaker is leaving an awful relationship, and he or she shies away from developing serious relationships or simply prefers to remain single. Our hero eventually decides they are ready to reengage that part of life. And their first attempts are quite awkward. They pick someone who makes you, their friend, question their sanity. Or they have too many walls built up; they seem to be walking around concussed from smashing into their own defenses."

Cliff and numerous audience members chuckled and nodded their heads at the description. Brian sat back, a look that balanced contentment and delight on his face. He loved the moments without lights, video, or any particular fanfare when Michael spoke to a crowd, and the connection that was made became a physical presence in the room. From a professional level, it meant priceless word-of-mouth advertising for his client. From a personal standpoint, he just found it fun to watch. Sara, who was seated next to him, nodded with the crowd. She and Brian had discussed on numerous occasions Michael's ability to connect with his audiences. Despite seeing this phenomenon before, she was still slightly surprised he could do it in a room of three hundred when she was still nervous to present information to a room of fifteen.

"I can see that Cliff's question has led to a deeper understanding for quite a few of you. That's a good thing. You see, Cliff," Michael pointed at his latest favorite pupil, "when you take the time to express an idea or question, you never know who you're going to help. It's a wonderful thing. I do think, however, it's time to give someone else the floor."

Cliff was losing himself in thought but managed to haphazardly mumble "Okay" and return to his seat, his mind not quite reconnecting with his body. While he pulled a copy of Michael's book from his backpack and found some pages he desperately needed to reread, a man in his early fifties stepped to the microphone, opting to stand as he spoke. He was unshaven, and there were noticeable bags under his eyes. He seemed burdened and lacked the energy Cliff had brought to the proceedings. Michael, who had returned to his seat, suspected the listlessness had little to do with age, though he did not presume to know its source.

"Hello," the man muttered in a restrained voice. "I feel kinda bad asking this"—*But you will anyway*—"but don't you feel at all hypocritical?"

Some audience members groaned when they heard the question. Others looked quickly at Michael, as if they were no longer in a lecture hall but watching a tennis match. Michael leaned back in his chair and rubbed his chin. He suppressed the grin that was fighting to crawl across his face. He was fascinated by the question. "Not sure why I should feel hypocritical. If you can explain why you think I should, I will explain if I agree with you."

"Well, you're up there talking about dating. You talk in your book about the importance of relationships, and yet you're divorced. From what I've read, you asked for the divorce. Who are you to tell anyone about the importance of relationships?"

My lord, you haven't heard a word I've said all night. Michael leaned forward in his chair and looked at the speaker, his smile no longer denied.

Sara glanced nervously at Brian. "What is he smiling about? This room is so tense right now."

Brian, knowing Michael very well, shook his head. "He's getting ready to write. The tension in the room? Shit, he doesn't even notice it. He is unfazed by what someone else might deem an insult."

"Getting ready to write? What do you—?"

"Fifteen years," Brian crowed, winking at his assistant. "Trust me. Trust him. It's all good."

"Well," Michael was still seated but leaning back again, "the short answer is no, not at all. I feel that way for any number of reasons. Would you like to hear one or two?"

"Sure."

"And your name is?"

"David."

"Hello, David. I am quite honestly glad you're here. When in my book or presentation did I claim to hold special wisdom or knowledge about marriage, relationships, or anything else?"

"Well, you didn't, but you talk about them."

"I assume by 'them' you mean relationships. I talk about them because they are important. Because they are part of being human. Maybe the most important part of being human. I talk about them, and I write about them. I do so, frankly, because I want to be better at them. All of them. The father, the friend, the writer, the presenter, the acquaintance, the uncle, and, yes, even those complicated romantic ones." Michael's confession circled the room on wings of authenticity, touching wounded hearts and other trembling minds. He continued, his tone still unassuming but certain, "But I am no expert, and I don't claim to be. I am, like I explained earlier tonight, a corridor."

"Yeah," David's cynicism rose like a tidal wave, "you said that. When you talk like that, I feel like you're pulling something."

"I'm just trying to be honest," professed Michael. "I am a corridor. I read the thoughts of a multitude of people, past and present, as I seek to understand what it means to live a flourishing life. If someone hears me and thinks I have something special to offer, they are likely mistaken. I try to create a corridor for my readers and listeners to experience the thoughts of titans. I am not such a person." *Far from it.* "I can, however, allow contact to take place with what I've read, if I can just let it all pass through me. Forget about me. It's the lessons. If something I say sounds helpful, try to apply it to your life. If not, seek elsewhere. If I claimed to be a relationship expert, I would, indeed, be a hypocrite. I am a seeker and a corridor. That's all."

"Okay," David said, turning to reclaim his chair. Or perhaps to leave the room altogether. Michael didn't know. He didn't care. He just knew the conversation wasn't over.

"How long ago did you get divorced, David?"

David turned back to the microphone. "Excuse me?"

"How long ago did you get divorced?" Michael repeated. He was still seated, but to many a person, he appeared to have grown in stature. "You come in here, angry at a stranger. Clearly filled with pain. Angry about the perception that I claimed special knowledge. Also, your unhappiness seems familiar to me. How long ago did you get divorced? If I am wrong, just tell me. It will hardly be the first time."

David hesitated. "A year."

"That's a tough year." Michael's sincere sympathy caused David to drop his head. "You think you know what you did wrong in the relationship, don't you?"

"Yes," David whispered looking up at Michael.

"And it pisses you off, knowing you needed a divorce to grasp how to be a better husband in a marriage? Even in your previous marriage?"

David swallowed hard but remained at the microphone. "Yes."

"Ain't that a kick in the teeth? Some of the things you told her she was wrong about, she was actually right about. But you can't go back and fix it, can you?"

"No, she's done."

"And you know more about making a relationship work now than you ever did before," Michael said. "I like to think I'm not a hypocrite, and I hope you know you're not one either. You're a human being learning about life. Learning doesn't end because we reach a certain age. We are just too stubborn to learn some lessons without a few bitter experiences."

"Maybe. How? I?" David's mouth opened, but no words were forth coming. His groping attempt to find words prompted Michael to speak quickly.

"We can speak later if you want to. Or not. Just seems to me like the wheels in your head are turning too fast for your mouth to keep up." Michael gazed at David for a moment. "I would say this before we part company. I bet your ex-wife made some mistakes, too. These things are rarely all one person's fault. Be careful blaming yourself for that which you are not guilty."

David nodded. He returned to his seat in silence. To his surprise, supportive clapping was smattered about the auditorium and strangers patted his shoulders as he trudged by.

"Well," Michael said, leaning back in his chair. "Next question! Evidently, we are open to all topics tonight."

CHAPTER 6
FRIENDLY DRINKS

Michael sat at the bar in Kells, an Irish pub some four blocks from the hotel. Needing some fresh air after the presentation, he strolled to the pub in a casual fashion. He was tired from the busy day yet dreaded trying to fall asleep. Perhaps some Bushmills Irish whiskey would be an effective sleep aid, he hoped. If it wasn't, well, that was fine, too. Michael did enjoy a good glass or three of Bushmills. He was just taking another sip when Sara exploded onto the chair next to him.

"Can you believe that guy? I mean, you handled it great, but what an ass!"

"Good evening," Michael deadpanned, ignoring her animated entrance. "So, how was your night?"

Sara rolled her eyes, waving at a group of imaginary companions, and groused, "Yeah, yeah. Pleasantries all around. C'mon, Michael! Wasn't that guy an ass? Why aren't you more bothered?"

"Well, I was going to get upset, but it seems you've got that covered for both of us. And Brian too, for that matter."

Sara tilted her head to the side, causing her black hair to fall to one shoulder. She looked up at Michael and sneered. "Aren't you hilarious? But seriously, not even a little annoyed?"

"Honestly," Michael began, trying not to drown in Sara's blue eyes, "I very quickly realized he was a man in pain. When that realization kicked in, what he was saying mattered little to me. Why was he saying it? Now that was a point of fascination. Made for a good moment in the Q&A though, right?"

"That it did," Sara somewhat reluctantly admitted while looking for the bartender. He quickly came over once she caught his eye. He took her order and busied himself in the mixing of the drink. "Great service here."

Michael couldn't tell if she was speaking to him or making a proclamation for the bartender to hear. "What are you getting?"

"Oh, some house cocktail. It sounded, hmmmm, filled with alcohol," Sara said, pulling her knees up to fit her entire body on the bar stool. The fact she was about 5'4" and slender made the odd contortion look semi-comfortable.

"Curling up to go to sleep?" Michael asked.

"No. I just have trouble sitting still."

"Or standing still. Or probably sleeping without thrashing. Do you sit when you eat, or do you just wander around the table?"

Sara pointed her finger at Michael and feigned anger. "Listen you, just because you had a good day doesn't mean I'll let you get away with mocking me."

"So you say." Michael took a sip of his whiskey. Sara's lime green concoction was placed before her, and Michael raised his glass. "To good days."

"Good days," Sara said, touching glasses. "By the way, I really liked that *Lion King* analogy you made. It was quite effective. Did it just pop into your head?"

"Glad it worked. As for it popping into my head, that would be a yes and a no. I used that concept—'All of life's problems can be solved with *The Lion King*'—in my classes. First time, I was just fumbling about, trying to find something to help connect the students to my material. The more I used it, the more it worked. Sometimes in surprising ways. Anyway, I did not plan on using it tonight, but it was comfortable to bring it out."

"It really worked. It should have been in the book." Sara's eyes widened as she amused herself at Michael's expense. "Make sure you do a better job writing the next one."

Michael chuckled at the lighthearted jab. "I'll keep that in mind. Maybe you could co-author."

"Yikes! It's hard enough pushing books uphill. I couldn't imagine writing one."

"The offer is on the table," announced Michael, slapping the bar for extra emphasis. "Was there any aspect of the *Lion King* riff you found particularly appealing?"

"Well, actually, it wasn't the analogy as much as what it led to. Which I suppose is the point. You were speaking with that young guy. You were talking about graceless lurching and clumsy attempts to go forward in life. That kinda resonated with me." Sara looked away from Michael. Far away from anything. She sipped her drink while gray clouds drifted across her eyes.

Michael watched her thoughts slowly return to the pub. If he were someone else, he may have changed the topic, but his inclination to stand in foul weather got the best of him. "Going through a rough spell? Feel free to borrow my ear. Or my shoulder. Whichever seems more helpful."

Sara released a muted sigh. "That's nice. I appreciate it. I really do."

"Well, yeah. Just don't get really happy about that, though. I mean, shit, I was nice to that asshole tonight, too!"

Sara laughed and then struck Michael's shoulder. "Wait a minute! Did you just put me in the same boat as that guy?"

"Not at all," Michael said through a barbed smile. "But I am curious about what resonated with you."

"Well, I had a bad breakup a little way back. That thing you mentioned about the breaker losing the ability to trust. I understand that."

"You broke it off with this guy?"

"Yes, I did," Sara boasted, clearly proud of her decision, "and I won't tell you anymore. At least not without a few more drinks."

"I get it. Some occasions just aren't right for discussing certain things. However, when discussing bad break ups, as well as some pointless second guessing, you need look no further than me. Hell, my ex-wife and I couldn't find common ground with a team of marriage counselors and a road map. Sometimes it was like we were speaking different languages and, believe me, I own a fair share of the blame."

"Ouch. So the whole lack of communication thing did you two in?"

"Not exactly. We tried to work through it, but other complications got in the way. Make no mistake, I am happier now." Michael hesitated, unsure what to share and what to hide. "I guess I'm just saying that I get it."

"You might. What were the other complications?"

"I won't tell you anymore, at least not without a few more drinks."

"Ha! You used my line," Sara laughed and leaned briefly into Michael. He was at least a foot taller than Sara, and he bent down as the two shared a laugh.

"Barkeep, more drinks!" Michael called to no one there.

"Yes!" Sara exclaimed. "Oh, lean back. I don't want the bartender to think we're together. He's cute."

"Don't think he's a bit young?"

"So am I," protested Sara. "Thirty-six is young."

"It is," Michael said. "How shall you get his attention?"

"Oh, that's easy. I'll just give him my look." Sara chewed knowingly on her straw with a slight grin. She tilted her head to look at Michael.

"That works?" Michael hoped his incredulous delivery covered up the fact he felt he was drowning in eyes that could not see him.

"Evidently only on young men. For someone like you, I would have to try something different." Sara walked her fingers three steps up Michael's arm and laughed.

The bartender interrupted the moment. "Can I help you two?"

"Another Bushmills," Michael said. "Rocks."

"Another Moher Mist for me," Sara requested, a broad smile accompanying the order.

"No problem." The bartender responded with a polite grin, a reward for Sara's efforts before dutifully turning to prepare the drinks.

"I think he's too beautiful for me," Sara confessed. "He probably gets hit on all the time."

"Could be, or he could just have shitty taste in women and therefore not realize he should be flattered," Michael said.

"Why, thank you." Sara held her almost empty glass aloft, waiting for Michael to join the toast. He did so, which bolstered her confidence. "Damn right he should! By the way, I should spend more time with you. It would do wonders for my self-esteem!"

"Well, I hope you enjoyed what you got because I have hit my compliment quota for the day. Besides, I don't want you getting a swelled head."

"I have many flaws," Sara conceded. "However, I don't think arrogance is one of them."

"Here ya go," the bartender said, placing the new drinks in front of them.

"These on the house?" Sara asked, tilting her head like she had demonstrated earlier.

"I don't have that power." The bartender moved down the bar to take another order.

"He lied," Sara sneered. "He could comp a drink if he wanted."

"C'est la vie," said Michael.

"Indeed. Where were we?"

"You're not arrogant."

"Yes! That's right!"

"Unlike Melissa from corporate headquarters?"

"God yes! Ugh. I can't stand her! I love it when you get under her skin. Love it!" Sara took a long sip of her drink.

"Glad I amuse. Are we meeting with her tomorrow?"

"No. Listen, don't get me wrong. I know she has a job and is actually very good at it. It just seems like she works in publishing but doesn't like books. Or writing. Or the writing process. Or authors."

"She is grounded in the business of publishing. You enjoy the art of writing," Michael proposed.

Sara smacked Michael's arm. "That's it! How did she even get to this phase of the business?"

"I have no idea," Michael said. "Honestly, I tease her in an attempt to show her the process can be enjoyed, not just the finish line."

"That's not working at all."

"That's true." The topic of Melissa having run dry, Michael steered the conversation to a far more fascinating subject. "Do you ever write?"

"Me? No. I mean, I think I would like to but just lack the dedication, I guess. I have ideas though."

"Write them down," encouraged Michael. "You might find that by simply writing the idea for a book, a book starts to be written."

Sara looked at Michael, her confidence in the idea momentarily rising before doubts dragged hope back to the depths. She answered in a noncommittal tone, "I'll try." She took a long sip of her drink followed by a longer one.

Michael consumed a healthy dose of whiskey. "It's a daunting process. The first step, I suppose, is don't give in to the fear generated by the horror of a blank page."

"Exactly," Sara blurted. "I look at one page, and all I can think is I need three hundred of these filled!"

"Holy shit! That is no way to get started!" Michael bellowed through a laugh.

"Tell me about it! You really seem to understand this. You should write a book sometime."

Michael chuckled and swirled the whiskey in his glass. "I'll think about it. Hey, we aren't meeting with Melissa tomorrow, but we are meeting, right?"

"Yes, we do have another morning powwow. It's scheduled for eight."

"I have to attend?"

"Yes. And no walking out like you did today. If I stay, you stay."

"Well, Melissa tends to be my motivation to leave, so with her out, I'll probably stick around."

Sara laughed again. "How very gracious of you."

A devilish grin grew as Michael schemed. "I could cut out just to piss off Brian."

"Nah," Sara rejected the idea outright, "wouldn't be the same."

"Probably not," Michael admitted. He took another sip of his Bushmills, his mind turning to Ireland. "Have you ever been to your drink's namesake?"

"What's that? Oh, the Cliffs of Moher. No, never been to Ireland."

"Well now, you need to cross that off your bucket list. It's beautiful. And calming. I found it quite relaxing. I traveled there after my divorce."

"Oh really? With someone?"

"Just me and my shattered psyche," Michael said with a bemused smile. "We need to get you there. You would fit right in."

"Because I'm beautiful?" Sara struck an innocent pose and batted her eyes.

"Maybe because you're calming. Wait, no. That's not it. That's not it at all."

Sara placed her hand over her heart as if mortally wounded. "Ouch. You are out of compliments."

"Only until midnight, then I can start again."

"That'll be in five minutes. I expect to hear something nice."

"I'll keep that in mind." The two friends finished their drinks before Michael spoke again. "Shall we get to going?"

"Sounds good," Sara said. "Another long day tomorrow."

"Yeah, so it goes." Michael settled his tab and walked after Sara, who was already meandering to the front door. "Can I walk out with you, or should I keep my distance just in case the bartender is watching?"

"Stay a couple steps behind. I'll let you know when to catch up," Sara teased.

The two exited the bar and proceeded back to the hotel. Sara allowed Michael to walk beside her after a couple of steps down the street, if only to pester him to grace her with another compliment. He happily complied.

Canst thou draw out leviathan with an hook?...Lay thine hand upon
him, remember the battle, do no more.
Behold, the hope of him is in vain: shall not one be cast down even
at the sight of him?...When he raiseth up himself, the mighty are
afraid...Upon earth there is not his like...
-a description of the leviathan from the Book of Job

CHAPTER 7
FACING A DEMON

That was unexpectedly pleasant. Michael entered his hotel room with a knot in his stomach as excitement and anxiety battled for supremacy in his heart and mind. Barely five minutes had passed since he walked Sara to her room. It was a good night, but one now burdened by the uncertainty of hopes and dreams. He had known Sara for over a year and seen her at various professional functions. This tour had allowed for increased contact and more personal interaction, which Michael was growing to enjoy more than he thought he would. *Could we? Would she be interested?*

He shook his head and laughed at himself. *That was way too comfortable. Or is that how it's supposed to be, and I've forgotten?* It was a small thing in essence, but he could not remember the last time he said goodnight to someone other than one of his two daughters. He brushed his teeth and climbed into bed. The next fifteen minutes were spent jotting thoughts in his journal. Fears of success and failure found their way onto the pages. The journal was returned to his nightstand when the knots in his stomach loosened and the dreams found anchors to the earth. Sighing, he checked the time. It was 1:05 a.m., a good time to pretend to fall asleep. Breaking his recent pattern, he fell quickly into a slumber. But the midnight demons came calling.

***

A desolate street stretched out before him; dilapidated buildings marked the existence of life from a shrouded era. Opened buildings were protected by mostly boarded windows, and not a single door was found on any hinge. Shuffling creatures, perhaps people, skulked about listlessly in some of the buildings—they moved as shadows, as wraiths, within the hollowed-out structures. Occasionally, one would stop at a rare open window and gaze at Michael, eyes accentuated by the filth each wore. Every careful glance carried a lifetime of despair.

Michael stood alone in a gentle rain. He sought in vain for one sign of companionship. All that came to him was litter and rubbish drifting in the wind. It was a slight breeze, the kind that informs of winter's approach. Decrepit streetlamps created weak pockets of light in the gloom. One building, a wooden church, stained glass windows long since shattered, was partially illuminated by the lamps. He took two steps toward the sacred space, dirt and mildew robbing the white paint of forgotten vibrancy. The building called forth the pain and disappointment of loss. The loss of what, however, Michael was uncertain. His stomach dropped as if word of a loved one's unexpected death was received. Tears swelled and he swallowed hard while the mysterious pain encompassed him. A skittering noise to his left broke his trance and called his attention.

In a window appeared a wraith, pointing down the street and emitting a low moan before disappearing from sight. The soulful lament acted like an alarm, and others did the same, now shrieking as they fled some unknown menace. Whatever physicality they had was absorbed by the black sky, darkness absorbing darkness, until all of them had dissipated. A low moan continued to drift on the air. It was unclear if it was the wind or the echoing calls of the undead. Ultimately, it was unimportant, for knowing the source would not have prevented the chill which ran the length of Michael's spine. Wrapping his overcoat tightly around his body, Michael looked down the street, shivering while he contemplated what caused the wraiths to flee. *Could it be? Oh god, no. Not him. Please not him. He's been gone so long.*

A hulking behemoth came into view. The concrete groaned with each footfall as he prowled the street in search of prey. The creature stood some eight feet tall and appeared to be made of earth and stone. Its head was little more than a rock skull protruding from a dirt-matted lump. Red eyes shone from beneath a crusted brow. The distance between shoulders was a terror unto itself; the beast's girth created the illusion of a moving mountain. Rocks covered the hands and arms, creating the sense of chaotically assembled armor. The chest was also covered by a slab of stone, as if the earth itself protected this beast. Vines ran like veins in the creature's legs and arms, some protruding outside the body. It could well have emerged whole and intact from some forgotten chasm, ancient as the primordial mystery of the universe. Every step was catastrophic and violent. The beast stopped its death march to growl at a lone wraith that remained in a window too long. The specter turned to dust and was dispersed by the increasingly intense wind.

Michael, who had been immobilized the moment he saw the beast, was freed to move when the wraith was dispatched. Leaden legs carried him into the closest building; all hopes hinged on finding a place of refuge. A place to hide. He entered an old gym where some remnants of former utility remained. Hanging listlessly on a chain was a heavy bag. Cobwebs entwined a speed bag, awaiting release. Yearning for one last moment of purpose. It would likely wait an eternity. In the corner of the room was a boxing ring. It may have been sturdy. The dim light from the streets allowed Michael to see boxing gloves, sawdust, and newspapers on the floor, celebrating long forgotten glory. Hiding places were few. It mattered little, for the time to seek sanctuary had passed.

The creature burst through the wall and roared. The building may have trembled more than Michael, though it could not back-pedal as he did; a futile action but the only action his trembling limbs allowed. The creature moved with speed that defied its mass. A massive fist thundered from the heavens, crushing Michael to the ground. He was all but shattered by a single blow. Michael was hauled to his feet for the creature's joy of delivering another murderous strike. Falling in a heap to the floor, he was helpless before this vortex of rage. Impotent before its power. The beast pulled Michael back up and held him aloft long enough to unleash a skull-shattering headbutt. Michael fell again, gasping for life.

The assault was unrelenting. Michael was effortlessly pulled close to the beast's face where he could not escape the flaming glare of his tormentor. There was no pity in those red eyes. Hate. Rage. Despair. They were all present. Michael cursed his weakness, his cowardice, while he was suspended in the grip of this demon. A rag doll with no choice but to endure what was happening.

Thrown as if by a hurricane, Michael sailed through a gaping hole the creature had left in the wall of the gym and came to rest in the street. Painfully, he rolled to his stomach. He groaned but did not rise. The winds now howled, and the misty rain was a torrent. The elements were far stronger than he. Desperate, Michael looked down the street and saw an alley with a dumpster at the corner. Maybe he could hide there. Michael pushed himself to a crawling position because he still could not find his feet. *Pathetic. Coward. Is this what you deserve?*

As if answering the unspoken question, the beast was upon him. Earthen muscles pulsed with energy, and Michael was jettisoned through another wall. He landed on the floor of a bedroom. A queen bed with dingy sheets dominated the long-neglected space. A woman lay on a dingy mattress, cobwebs clinging to graying black hair. She groaned, seeking aid from the failure on her floor. Michael could not find his voice when he struggled to his knees.

The beast entered the room and kicked Michael, sending him sailing into the wall. A filthy mirror on a bureau was shattered by the force of the blow, while the wardrobe in the corner rocked forward but held itself upright. Michael trembled on the ground before the wardrobe. The beast approached Michael, seeking a completion of its task. Hearing the woman whimper on the bed, it turned on her, lifting her up and holding her above its head. Michael wished there was something he could do other than watch helplessly while the monster ripped the woman in half, casually tossing body parts back on the bed.

Michael rolled onto his stomach, attempting to crawl away. To somehow escape. To where, he did not know. A stony foot on his back halted all progress. The creature pulled a vine out of its arm, which quickly found its way around Michael's neck. The beast pulled on his makeshift noose, bending Michael into a painful arch before pushing his head violently back to the floor.

Grabbing Michael's hair and belt, the creature hoisted him so he was suspended parallel to the floor, facing the wardrobe. *God, no! That's not a wardrobe. It's the Door! My Door! How is it here, far from its home in the pit? What is happening?*

Like a battering ram, Michael was pummeled repeatedly into the Door. Despite the beast's strength, the Door did not give way. Michael was bloodied beyond recognition. Teeth were smashed and his eyes swollen shut. The creature dropped him to the floor, seemingly disgusted at Michael's failure to breach the barrier. He was rolled onto his back, which allowed the creature to grab his throat. A fist was raised to deliver a final blow. The creature roared in celebration of its victory as death descended upon Michael.

***

Something between a gasp and a scream escaped Michael, and he sprang up in his bed. His heart pounded; his mind raced. Knots in his stomach made it difficult to draw a clean breath. Tears streamed down his cheeks. *Ohmygod. Ohmygod. Nightmare. You're okay. Just a nightmare. Oh my. Okay. Calm down. Calm down. Okay. Just a dream.* His breathing steadied while the knots unwound. The tears his sleep had pulled from him subsided as he grasped the simple fact he was awake. He left the bed and raced to his bathroom where he poured a glass of water, drank it quickly, and poured another. He returned to the bedroom and sat on the floor, attempting to gather his thoughts. One question dominated his mind. *Why are you back?*

You are invited to stay in the house of the Tathagata, but your habit
energy makes you sleep night after night among the reeds.
-King Tran Thai Tong as quoted by Thich Nhat Hanh in *Living*
Buddha, Living Christ

CHAPTER 8
A BIGGER STAGE

The soulless beep of a mechanical alarm emanated from Michael's cell phone. He stood at the window of his hotel room, gazing on the scene below him while the morning sun gently illuminated the streets below, and ignored the technological summons. The manicured lawns of other hotels, the highway leading out of town, a Roman Catholic Church, various shops, chain restaurants, and a local diner were all bathed in the radiance of the new day.

Stepping away from the window, he lifted his mobile device from the night table and shut off the unnecessary alarm. Sleep was a stranger since his nightmare. He paused to look at the glass of watery whiskey, which also made its home near his bed, and finished the diluted contents. How long had he stood in front of the window? He had no idea. A morning meeting, however—*that* he remembered. Sara had mentioned it the night before. Enjoying time in the bar with her seemed to have occurred months, not hours, ago. The memory of his nightmare now dominated his mind. *Why are you back?*

Michael sighed as he strode into the living space of the room and sat down on the sleeper sofa, still holding his cell phone. He stared at it for a moment. *Text Sara. It will brighten my mood. No. She can't be responsible for.... She needn't know about this. It's not her job. It's mine. Mine alone. She need not know about this dark place. No one does.* Despite himself, Michael pulled Sara's number up on his cell. The sight of her name calmed his racing mind. He pulled a deep breath into his lungs and slowly exhaled. *Don't be a fool.* A slight smile temporarily rose without his consent, visiting his face for a nanosecond before fading. The feeling it rode remained a bit longer. A slight chuckle and he placed the phone on a coffee table.

Leaning back in the sofa, Michael consciously returned his thoughts to his dream. And his exhaustion. He needed to delve into the nightmare. Despite fatigue and fear, he felt compelled to do so. *Driven to the wilderness. Stop that!* Why was he having it again? What did it signify? What was happening? Michael moved to the edge of the sofa and planted his feet firmly on the ground. His hands were placed in his lap, palms up, fingers of his left hand laid across his right. With eyes closed, he drew a deep breath, in through his nose and out of his mouth. He let his body decide when the next breath was needed. The tip of his tongue touched the gumline just above his upper incisors. All his attention zeroed in on this spot, and his thoughts slowed. So he sat, straining for serenity, for the next ten minutes.

Far from calm but a safe distance from frantic, Michael rose. His initial instinct, to skip the morning meeting and call Brian for an update, was scrapped. This would cause more harm than good. Missing the meeting would require an explanation. A lie. One that Brian would likely not believe, which would create questions and unwanted conversation. Far better, Michael concluded, to attend the meeting. Maintain the expected schedule. Muster up some good spirits and proceed with the day. That will work. Given the lack of sleep over the past weeks, whatever sense others had of his festering anxiety could be blamed on weariness. That was hardly a stretch. *Alright. Get ready. Get coffee. Get game face on. Get to the meeting. That'll do.*

Michael showered quickly and threw on a pair of jeans and gray T-shirt. No need to dress in anything more than usual. He exited the room and then returned to put his shoes on. Content with his casual attire, Michael left again to procure his morning coffee. He was the last one to enter Brian's suite, not out of the ordinary for him.

"Good morning, Michael," greeted Brian politely and pointed at his client's feet. "Thanks for dressing up for us."

"No problem. I figured since Melissa wasn't here, I would show up in my professional attire."

"Well, I'm honored." Brian looked at the screen on his cell phone.

Michael took the chair next to Brian's assistant. "Morning, Sara."

"Morning. Ready to face another day as the superstar writer?"

"Easy," Michael cautioned, "my self-esteem can't handle that kind of praise. Besides, isn't today's schedule pretty light?"

Brian circled around a sofa to join them. "It is. I must confess that I'm slightly amazed to hear you're even aware of the schedule."

"I pay attention to things," Michael proclaimed, selling his false indignation. "I'm pretty sure these meetings and schedules have something to do with my life, after all. Tomorrow's schedule is light as well, if memory serves."

"Wow, you are the height of locked-in and organized. Put a pair of shoes on you and suddenly you can run your own company," Sara marveled sarcastically.

"Only with the right people next to me," responded Michael with an extra touch of cheer.

"Okay," Brian said. "Let's focus just a little, people. You have a signing session at a bookstore some thirty minutes from here. That is at 4:30. You then have an evening presentation...."

Sara, noticing Brian's searching pause, interjected, "7:00."

"Yes, 7:00. Thank you. The convention center is about ten minutes from the bookstore."

"Smooth sailing," Michael said. "This centrally located hotel is helpful. I like having a home base from whence to launch our daily marketing assault."

Sara looked at Michael and winced. "'From whence to launch?' Who talks like that?"

"I'm a writer. I was taking my," Michael paused to add comedic drama, "poetic moment."

"I wish you would take a nap," Brian deadpanned, "or at least like our home base enough to sleep through the night."

"Well, don't schedule these meetings so early, and I would."

Brian groaned dryly, "Yeah, that's the problem. Actually, this meeting is early because I just wanted to go over a couple of things with the three of us here before Sara hits the road."

"Leaving our merry band?" Michael asked, looking into Sara's pale, blue eyes.

"Not permanently. Just taking advantage of the lull to go home for three days to spend some time with my son. He misses his mommy."

"And mommy, no doubt, misses him," offered Michael. "It's good you're taking this opportunity. Time can go fast."

"I do miss him. And I'm worried my mother and father might write me out of the will if I don't give them a little time off! I do, however, expect an update regarding your meeting with Melissa."

"Melissa? What's going on?" Michael asked quickly. Sara's tone left him feeling displaced. "We have something new on the table?"

"Well, you know how we three and Melissa discussed the idea of a weekend retreat with you? With writing seminars and more detailed discussions regarding your book?"

"Well, of course. I thought that was already scheduled."

"It is," Sara said, "but now one of your full group presentations has been opened to the public at large. It is going to be recorded and played on PBS and broadcasted on NPR. Promotional packages including a DVD of the event, a couple of keepsakes, and discounts for our next book will be made available. I think Melissa would like your presentation for the DVD to be a bit more, let's say theatrical."

Michael groaned. "Let me guess. They want a stage with props and some kind of movie screen behind me?"

"Yup," confirmed Brian.

Sighing, Michael continued. "State of the art sound system to blast out some lyrics?"

"Hell, yes!" Sara exclaimed, striking Michael's shoulder. "It'll be fun! Your presentations are great, but they are a bit acoustic. You could kinda rock out a little bit!" Sara was now on her feet, her hands in motion as she visualized the new stage.

"I see." Michael hoped a nod of his head would disguise his listless tone. Sara and Brian both offered him incredulous looks. "Hey! I get it. I actually do. I'm serious. I just don't want the interaction I tend to have with my smaller audiences to get lost in a production. That's important to me." He emphasized the word important.

"I know it is. That may have to be sacrificed for this event, Michael," counseled Brian.

"Or you can take it as a challenge!" Sara declared, vibrating with energy. She stared into the distance, pointing at an unseen horizon. "I mean, your guy, Springsteen. He reaches the last seat in the auditorium. The people way up in the nosebleed section feel like they're in the middle of the action! What if you could do that?"

"That would be something." Michael leaned forward. "But I don't know if I can." *I'm not that good. I'm just me.*

Sara was suddenly quite earnest. "Don't sell yourself short. Don't."

"The auditorium has two thousand seats, and the aim is to fill it." Brian was becoming infected by Sara's enthusiasm. "Fewer than the Boss usually works."

"And a much bigger room than I'm used to," Michael countered. "If I do this, I will need to write a different script in order to incorporate more video and music."

"And lights!" Sara exclaimed, posing as if in a spotlight before continuing to migrate about the room.

Michael laughed despite his nerves, eyes lingering on Sara's movements a heartbeat longer than he intended before looking at Brian. "You two do realize I was a college professor before this book took off? What you're talking about is well beyond any vision I had for presentations."

Sara waved her hand to dismiss the thought. "So what? You were probably one of those absentminded professors who was a little whacky. Just be that—only bigger!"

Michael looked skeptically at Brian. *Bigger? I'm already too far beyond myself.*

"Don't look at me," Brian said. "She's got your number."

"Great," groused Michael. "This is still a bit down the road, right?"

"Yes, but Melissa is coming in to meet with us tomorrow, so you need to keep wrapping your mind around it."

"Can do, boss."

"I know you can. Tell you what: take some time and process this event. Jot down some notes. Get neurotic and, in the end, get comfortable with it all. I will text you the specifics for the bookstore visit today just in case I don't meet you here. But I should be back. Sara, I'll take you to the airport and get you on your way.

Text me your return itinerary."

"I did that yesterday," Sara said.

"Yeah, well, please do it again. I've been spending too much time with Michael and picked up some bad habits."

Sara laughed quietly to herself. Almost to herself. "You deleted it."

"Why, yes, I did. Just help me out. Anyway, I will pick you up from the airport if I'm available. And Michael, take a nap if you can. You need one."

"Tough to plan an event in my sleep," Michael retorted.

"Have a helpful dream," Sara suggested emphatically. "Lights! Music! Rock star!"

It was Michael's turn to laugh. "I will try. Have a nice trip, Sara."

"I will. You got this!"

"Yeah," Brian patted Michael's shoulder, "you got this."

"Sure thing," was the best answer Michael could find. He watched the two walk down the hall. *A helpful dream. What would that even look like?*

If one has not been a ronin at least seven times,
he will not be a true retainer.
Seven times down, eight times up.
-Yamamoto Tsunetomo, *Hagakure*
(Translator William Scott Wilson)

CHAPTER 9
THE ONLY WAY OUT

"I really loved the book. I'm a huge Springsteen fan." The speaker was a fifty-some-odd-year-old man, the last person in line seeking an autograph.

Michael sat at a table located in the bakery section of a Barnes & Noble. The area had been set up for a book talk and a meet and greet with readers. Michael was loath to call them fans, for who was he to have fans? "We all should be," Michael responded, pleased to acknowledge the true star of the book. "Who am I signing this for?"

"I'm Kurt," the man said. "Just sign anything. You're the writer, after all."

While the comment was good-natured and heard quite often over the past five weeks, it still made Michael feel pressure, as if he was supposed to come up with something pithy and profound. "From one Bruce fan to another" was scrawled before he added a line from a Springsteen song and signed his name in an illegible flourish. He returned the book to its enthused owner.

Kurt read the inscription and smiled. "Hey! You slipped a little 'Born to Run' in there. Nice touch!"

"Glad you like it," Michael responded warmly. "Take care."

Kurt waved and disappeared into the bookshelves. A few patrons lingered on the edge of the bakery. Perhaps they were waiting to speak with Michael or for the counter to reopen. The event manager whispered some instructions to a pair of young employees and made her way to Michael, who was patting his pockets looking for his keys.

"You lose something?"

"Nope." Michael pulled his keys from his pocket. "I am all set, Lisa. Thanks for your help. That went well."

"Yes, it did. We very much appreciate you coming here. It's nice to still have events like this."

Michael stepped to the side of the space to allow the employees to reset the floor. An inner delight rose and found a home in his eyes. "I love these events. I've done webinars and such things, and I know people like them. But to look the audience in the eye, especially a small crowd surrounded by books, for us to have the experience and opportunity for that personal connection, I will always have time for the brick-and-mortar store."

Smiling in agreement, Lisa nodded contentedly. "I feel the same way. Are you sure you don't need anything?"

"I'm good. Just going to grab an iced tea and unwind before my presentation down the road. I need to be there soon."

"Well, good luck, Professor. Thanks again. Keep us in mind for your next book."

"No doubt," Michael promised and offered a polite wave. He purchased an iced green tea and sat in a plush chair. His cell phone said it was 5:40; plenty of time to get to his next stop. He had already swung by the convention center to perform his ritual walk through. Having claimed the space, he was at ease with the idea of showing up as late as 6:30. No cameras. No lights. Acoustic. The thought had the power to simultaneously soothe and invigorate, causing Michael to chuckle softly to himself when he sent Sara a text.

How are things? Good flight?
To his surprise, she responded instantly.
Everything was smooth. I was just thinking of you. Ready for presentation?

Yup. Still at bookstore but leaving soon.
Still at bookstore? Get moving!
I've got time. How's your boy?
He's great! Engaged with Legos at the moment. He, un-like some others, is right where he should be.

Very subtle. Would it make you feel better if I told you I am going to scrap my planned presentation and go completely off the cuff?

What!? Are you trying to give me an anxiety attack? Are you nuts!
Not nuts. Thought I was a rock star!
Ha! Rock stars have playlists. Don't tell me more. I don't want to know. Just do a good job.
I will. Don't worry. Have a nice night.
You too.

Michael pocketed his phone and drove to the convention center. He had been issued a pass to the executive parking area, granting him an unhindered arrival. Brian, tapping his foot and fidgeting with his watch, greeted him in his dressing room. "It's 6:30. Are you kidding?"

"About what?"

"About what?" Brian repeated. "You're on in thirty minutes. Shouldn't you have been here sooner?"

"Why? To make you less nervous? I'm good to go."

"So you say. Oh, and what's this text I received from Sara? Are you actually planning on going off the cuff tonight? I don't think this is the time to just try out new material."

"You really think I 'just try out' anything without thinking about it first? Besides, I did write the book. It's not like I'm going out there completely from left field."

"Of course. I know that, but there is a pattern to these presentations. People sign up to attend based on what we advertise the night's focal point will be. They could be disappointed if they came expecting one thing and heard something else."

"Oh." Michael's grin grew slowly on his face, walking the often undefined border between confidence and cockiness, "they won't be."

Recognizing the futility of continued conversation, Brian stated, "I'm going to take my place in the back of the room. Do a good job."

The only reassurance he received was a wink from Michael. Brian took his place and counted seconds.

After fifteen minutes, Michael strode onto the stage with a gait that was quicker, more forceful, than his norm. Sauntering, sometimes almost wandering, into the space before the audience was how Michael usually made his appearance, like a good friend arriving to extend an invitation for a stroll. Not tonight. Tonight, his footfalls demanded you walk with him. This was no invitation; it was instruction. Brian drew a deep breath.

What was normal was the presence of a podium, a coffee table, and a comfortable chair on the stage. This was all Michael ever wanted. Notes were located on each of these furnishings, high-lights of the presentation that Michael wanted to be reminded of should, or more precisely when, he became sidetracked.

"Good evening, everyone," Michael said as he hit the center of the stage. "Always, and I mean always, a great pleasure to thank you all for coming out tonight. You're all adults. You all have busy schedules and for you to choose to spend that time here, with me, I appreciate it. I really do.

"But I've got a little problem tonight. Just a little one. You see, while I was walking the sidewalk to enter this facility, I heard some dogs howling at the moon. I don't know if I was on Main Street, but I know a good howl." Michael licked his lips after he alluded to Springsteen's "The Promised Land." Heads in the audience nodded, some in unison with him. "And you know what they were telling me? I need to own this moment. So, I am sorry, but I am changing the topic of tonight's presentation. You came expecting one thing, but I think I got something better for ya!" Michael stomped to the podium and crumpled the notes that were carefully prepared and placed for him. "And if it's not, well, if you feel disappointed, just speak to me after our talk, and we will get you a refund. Right, Brian? I'm sure Melissa won't mind!

"Alright," Michael clapped his hands together before quickly pointing at the crowd. "As you know, those dogs were, in essence, rooting for me to face the storms and uncertainty of my life.. That's what I want to talk to you about tonight. That fundamental idea that somewhere, for all of us, is a storm, threatening to rip our homes from their foundation. To turn our minds inside out. Hail and thunder hitting us so hard, our courage becomes cowardice, and we can feel lost in the flood.

"This concept shows up again and again in Springsteen's lyrics and in our lives. He also stresses the necessity to keep moving.

But it's a tough, tough walk. We see it in 'Badlands' where the idea that chasing our dreams can be downright terrifying is presented. Tonight, we are gonna talk about that fear. The possible sources and the possible solutions. It can be a frightening journey. I know it. And the time to start that journey is now.

"You see, I relate, like many do, to the idea that we all have baggage that weighs us down. We all have bags. Parts of ourselves that maybe we wish we could put down. Parts of ourselves that make us say, 'Once I deal with these bags, I will deal with the storm.' No. That's not the way to go! Even if you think it is, life won't let you. You got to head into the storm with everything you got—right now! And I mean right now! You got to head into that darkness, and maybe, just maybe, by going into the darkness, you can be liberated from whatever anchor has been dragging you down. Maybe by fighting the storm, you'll find out what you need to keep and what you can let go of. Maybe the storm can cleanse as well as destroy. Maybe at the end of the walk through the darkness, you'll feel your soul finally rise!"

Michael finished the statement with a flourish, his hand in the air like he was a testifying preacher. His attempt to continue the thought was interrupted by a spontaneous cheer from the crowd.

"Some folks are with me!" Michael shouted. In truth, the room was with him. They were an engaged community, the sincere speaker and the active listeners. An emotional journey had begun and while miles would not be consumed, enrichment might well be found. Brian stood in the back looking at Michael as if for the first time. He wasn't sure what prompted this presentation style, but he welcomed it, even as he cursed the fact he hadn't been recording it from the start.

"Stick with me now because I'm afraid that things might get a little confusing. That's all right though, for help is on the way. But it's not just us. I can tell you this: Confucius is on his way. Buddha is on his way. Archetypal images and Samwise Gamgee are on the way. I'm not sure when they'll arrive, but they're coming!"

No one was completely sure what Michael was talking about, but they knew, without a doubt, that somehow it would all make sense eventually. The next hour was a blur of enthusiasm, exaltation, and evaluation. Somehow in the whirlwind of the presentation, Michael settled the crowd into contemplative silence while at other times they burst into unexpected applause. Brian swore he saw a couple of people shed a tear or two, as if some chain deep within them shook and, perhaps, was even shattered. The time allotted for his presentation wound down and Michael took a seat on the edge of the stage, his legs dangling toward the floor. He leaned forward to speak to the audience; at times, his torso gave the appearance of a diver preparing to spring headlong into a pool.

"I just want to finish the night by returning to a concept I brought up earlier. It seemed a bit of a surprise to some of you, and I do value clarity. I mentioned the wrathful Buddhas of the Tantric and Tibetan tradition. People can become entangled in either/or thinking, believing if I am this, then I can't be that. For example, 'If I am spiritual, I must be peaceful.' I know some people like to consider themselves spiritual and not religious. That's fine. But I am concerned that people can use spiritual imagery or concepts to avoid going into the darkness or consider some parts of their humanity not spiritual and, therefore, put on airs of peace or tranquility while they strain to keep their heads above water."

Michael pulled himself to his feet while he spoke. His hands rotated in front of him, making five complete resolutions before he stopped them. He occasionally paused as he searched for words. "I love the idea of the wrathful Buddha. Those Buddhas who embraced the energies and emotions we call bad—anger, doubt, fear—and used them to drive into the darkness and, by so doing, overcame. Transformed, I think, would be more apt. We have Avalokitesvara, a wonderfully compassionate Buddha, who had an almost demonic, wrathful side called Mahakala who, ultimately, protected—and perhaps still protects—that which is precious. There was Yamantaka, the slayer of death, who demonstrated that death itself is not superior to the enlightened mind. The energy created by anger can be put to good use clearing paths so that peace and compassion may reign supreme. Anger, like the dew of morning, dissipates in the light of our growing sense of authenticity and compassion. Maybe the only way to freedom from the shadow is by going straight through."

Michael paused, deeply considering his statement while failing to ignore the tight knot which gripped his stomach. *Hypocrite.* Breaking his own trance he continued. "Thanks for the time. Anyone for some questions and answers?"

Ten people wasted no time heading for the microphone stands.

The skillful traveler leaves no traces of his wheels or footsteps;
the skillful speaker says nothing that can
be found fault with or blamed...
In the same way the sage is always skillful at saving men,
and so he does not cast away any man; he
is always skillful at saving things,
and so he does not cast away anything.
-Lao Tzu, *Tao Te Ching*, chapter 27

If you see an intelligent man who tells you
where true treasures are to be found,
who shows what is to be avoided, and administers reproofs,
follow that wise man; it will be better, not worse,
for those who follow him.
-The Buddha, *The Dhammapada*, chapter 6

CHAPTER 10
UNEXPECTED GREETINGS

A cup of coffee. Sunlight dancing a perfect waltz across a tranquil pond. A breeze just strong enough to push one's hair but not the thermostat. This morning was a simple pleasure, gifting Michael with an unfamiliar sense of serenity. It was 11:00 a.m. and already a good day. He was seated in Mary's Diner, nursing a second cup of coffee and considering how to factor his lounging into the tip. He was most certain that the lull in his schedule added to the calm that enveloped him. He was grateful that nature had decided to deliver a masterpiece on his day off and for the unexpected conversation the morning had produced.

As for official business, the only item on his agenda over the next thirty-two hours was a meeting with Brian and Melissa at 3:00 that afternoon. Brian wanted to talk at least thirty minutes prior to seeing Melissa. Actually, Michael suspected that Brian wanted to talk right that moment. The two had barely spoken after the previous night's presentation, because Michael was engaged in conversation with audience members for a full hour and a half after his presentation ended. To his disappointment, but not his surprise, the ongoing successes of the book tour did not bring a good night's rest. He slept for, perhaps, three hours before waking to the encompassing blanket of silence present at 3:30 in the morning.

From that point on, he rotated through a pattern of activities that included simply lying in bed, writing in his journal, getting up to stare out the window, sipping some whiskey, and lying on the floor for no particular reason at all (he told himself it was good for his back) before returning to bed in an attempt to sleep. Annoyed with this ineffective ritual, he vacated the hotel at 6:30 for a morning walk.

Thoughts of breakfast danced in his head when he sauntered past Mary's Diner on the corner, but a beautifully maintained park across the street beckoned. His stride, unrushed by any pressing deadlines, was nearly as casual as the ducks skimming along the pond. The wake of their passing spread expansively behind them until it dissipated, swallowed by the waters, leaving no evidence of their path.

Michael continued along the footpath that circled the park. He crossed a bridge and turned up a small flight of stone stairs. At the park's north end, the path forked: one route continued on and the other allowed passage back to the world. A small Catholic church, visible from Michael's vantage point, stood across the street. He looked at the building for the instant between breaths and found himself examining the arched wooden doors at the entrance. The polished wood stood in contrast to the white stone of the building itself, drawing Michael's eye and, eventually, his feet to the church's entry.

Five steps carried visitors from the sidewalk to the door. It was a simple entrance. Inviting even. Not a feeling Michael often associated with churches, even if he did admire their craftsmanship. He ran his fingers along the door, and a knot in his stomach ran across his torso, becoming a claw reaching into his chest.

"I'm afraid the door is locked until a bit later."

Startled, Michael turned quickly, tottering just a bit on the top stair.

"Whoa! Easy, my friend," the man exclaimed, reaching out his arms as he approached.

Regaining his physical balance, Michael spoke quickly in order to find his emotional equilibrium. "I'm fine. No worries. Just a little startled. I thought I was alone."

"Well, you were alone. Now you're not. I'm Father Sylvan," the priest offered his hand in greeting.

Michael descended the stairs to shake it. His demeanor grew calmer as he reached the pavement. "I'm Michael. This is a lovely church."

Father Sylvan bowed slightly at the waist. "Thank you. I built it myself. My boss, after all, was a carpenter's son. Glad you appreciate my workmanship."

Michael chuckled. "You're a fine craftsman, Father. Wait a second. Do I know you?"

"Not well, Mr. Tanner, but we have met. Yesterday to be precise."

"Ha! You were the last person in line at Barnes & Noble yesterday." Michael bit his lip and rubbed his brow. "Kurt! Your name is Kurt."

"Indeed, it is. I also listened to you speak last night at the convention center. You were doing some preaching, Professor. You sure you didn't miss your calling?"

Michael laughed again. "I think not. My ruminations take me a bit beyond the church."

"Mine too. Mine take me all the way to the Jersey shore and E Street!" Father Sylvan replied with a deep belly laugh that may have shaken his very soul. The joy accompanying the comment demanded Michael join in the laughter. His mirth subsiding, Father Sylvan continued. "I really like your book. And a lot of what you said last night. I can see where your work could be helpful to a great many people."

Do you? What do you see? "Did you? That's interesting."

"If you say so," a perplexed Father Sylvan replied. "What's interesting about it?"

"Nothing. I'm sorry," Michael mumbled, shaking his head and ambling toward the street. "I've likely wasted enough of your time. Have a good day."

Father Sylvan watched Michael take but one step before extending an invitation. "Actually, I was just going for my morning walk. You could join me for a lap or two around the park."

"Sure. Sorry I dismissed your interest."

"Are you Catholic?" Father Sylvan asked when the duo crossed the street.

Confused and reflexively defensive, Michael's answer crossed his lips with a hint of distrust. "No. Why do you ask?"

"You've just apologized twice when there was no need to. Unnecessary guilt is a very Catholic trait."

"Maybe." Michael was embarrassed by his gut reaction. "I have found guilt to be a very human trait. So, what did you like about last night's presentation, Father?"

"You're kidding me, right? Springsteen's music is filled with

Christian imagery, and you were hitting at those ideas pretty hard."

"True, but I never explicitly used any Christian references."

"I know. You did a great job, though, taking lyrics and weaving them seamlessly with some Eastern ideas and then bringing them forward to modern examples. How long did it take you to write that presentation?"

"Truth be told, I was almost completely off the cuff last night."

"No kidding," Father Sylvan mused, his voice drifting on a comforting wind. "That is fantastic. But how long have you worked to get to the point you can see a presentation unfold before your eyes and follow it with that kind of confidence?"

Michael scratched his head, considering the question. Not quite sure of his response, Michael decided to speak rather than think his way to an answer. "I probably reached that point about four years ago. In my youthful arrogance, I thought I was there over a decade ago, but I can see the quantum leap in the connective webs I perceived and communicated over the past four years. Well, maybe three."

"It's quite a talent you have. As for explicit Christian references, c'mon. I've known you for barely fifteen minutes, and I know you're better than that. Heading into storms, facing the darkness, rising above, moving from a state of weariness, perhaps spiritual weariness, to, at the least, a place where hope can be seen again. I'm fairly certain my tradition hits on those topics once or twice."

"Indeed, they do, Father. I suppose I wanted to introduce people to some ideas they may not be familiar with, therefore I headed east."

"I see. Allow me two comments. First, most people are as unfamiliar with the heart of Christianity as they are with works you utilize—"

"Are you pitching a project on me, Father?" Michael asked through a wry smile.

"Ha! No, but if you feel inspired, go with it!"

"Duly noted."

"Very good. Now my second comment," Father Sylvan cleared his throat and sang a couple of lines from Springsteen's "Adam Raised a Cain." He stopped after a couple more lines and offered his defense. "Hey, you said east. You triggered my memory, so I am blaming you for that."

"I will gladly accept that burden," Michael stated. He noted they were now across the street from Mary's Diner. "Y'know what, Father? I am going to go sit down in Mary's and get some breakfast. Care to join me?"

Father Sylvan sighed and held his protruding stomach. "I would love to, but I ought not to. If you find yourself craving some company over a coffee sometime, I'm in."

"You can't get coffee at Mary's?"

"Oh, you can get coffee. And home fries. And pancakes. And bacon. And, I think you get the point."

"Understood," Michael said, extending his hand. "It was a pleasure meeting you again, Father."

"Likewise. If you want that coffee come find me at St. Jude."

"St. Jude?" *How perfect.*

"Yes. You okay?" Compassion hung on Father Sylvan's voice. "A thought seemed to flash behind your eyes."

Michael shook his head. "No, nothing wrong. Just appreciating your patron saint."

"Lost or impossible causes? A final friend standing loyally with one on the brink of despair? You appreciate this?"

"I guess I'm just the kind of guy who doesn't think you can get to the mountain top without truly experiencing the valley, Father."

"I see. I think you are well-named." Father Sylvan paused a moment. "Peace be with you, Michael."

Michael smiled and waved, "And also with you."

He watched Father Sylvan walk away. *Michael. St.Jude. Mahakala.*

Stop! You're not a mystic. Entering Mary's Diner, he was greeted by a friendly waitress who pleasantly informed him to sit where he pleased. He settled into a booth, and his cell phone buzzed with an incoming message. It was Brian.

> Where are you? We need to talk.
> Out walking. We will. Back in two hours.

That should satisfy or at least hold him off. The cell buzzed again. Michael was pleased to see Sara's name appear on his phone, even if she was texting to chastise him.

> What did you do? Brian is beside himself.
> All went well. Brian is excited, not angry.
> That might be true but he's still pestering me! Get him off my back!
> No problem, whirlwind. What are you up to?
> I will be making breakfast without interruption when you handle Brian.
> Got it. Whatcha making?
> Chocolate chip pancakes.
> Mom of the year!
> I could be! I have to get back to it!
> Alright. Have a great day.
> You too.

Michael looked at the omelet and home fries that arrived at his table. *Have a good day? I think I've already had one.*

CHAPTER 11
THROUGH A STRANGER'S EYES

Father Sylvan looked over his shoulder and watched Michael enter the comfortable confines of Mary's Diner. The priest rubbed his stomach in an attempt to battle against his craving for home fries and loaded scrambled eggs. "Lead us not into temptation," was mumbled through a light chuckle. An amused shake of his head and he ordered his aging legs to continue along the park's path until he reached the north exit. From there, he completed his walk to the rectory where he would prepare a far less satisfying meal.

Breakfast, consisting of a bowl of Special K, a banana, and a strawberry yogurt was put on a tray to be carried to his favorite recliner. He just needed to wait for the Keurig to finish his coffee. Looking to the top of the refrigerator, he spied a bottle of Bailey's Irish Cream. A sigh escaped his lungs, if not his soul, as the door was pulled open and a container of half and half was procured. His breakfast was now fully assembled, so he moved to his throne, placed the tray on a coffee table, and sat. The first spoonful of Special K was hardly consumed before his thoughts turned to Michael. Something in their brief interaction had sparked his curiosity.

Brow furrowed, Father Sylvan leaned back into his recliner. On certain days, this action was little more than the precursor to a nap, but his mind was far too busy for such relaxation. Michael's reaction to the mention of St. Jude held his attention. Having counseled countless people and being a trusted source of encouragement to others made him particularly attentive to both the words people spoke and the manner in which those words were delivered. An inner cloud seemed to darken Michael's face when St. Jude was said. What was the word Michael used? Appreciated? Yes, appreciated. It was not a throwaway line. A fire burned in the author's eyes when he utilized the familiar imagery of mountaintops and valleys. What valley had Michael been in? How far had he climbed out of his personal pit? For he seemed to be doing well, despite a certain reluctance to accept compliments.

That was another aspect of Michael that stuck with Father Sylvan. It was not the typical angst one occasionally finds in artistic types. Writers, painters, musicians, sculptors—all of them seemed to carry a certain inner turmoil. Michael's was different. He had recoiled from a simple compliment like a man pulling back from having a wound prodded. There was something brewing in the author, concealed but swirling about. A personal battle of one type or another that Michael would need to face. What the battle was, he did not know. Would he be called on to be an ally, or was a chance meeting at St. Jude and a pleasant stroll the extent of his role in this particular tale? Time, the great thinner of things, would reveal the answer to such questions. A bite of soggy Special K and a sip of still warm coffee almost shook Michael from his mind, but there was something else.

Grunting, Father Sylvan rocked himself to his feet and circled the room to his work desk. He pulled open the top drawer on the right side, revealing a small notebook utilized for personal notes. It was with him the night he saw Michael's presentation. Flipping through the pages, he found the name he sought: Mahakala. What an interesting concept, that of the wrathful Buddha.

Placing the notebook back in the desk, the priest moved to the bookshelf on the opposite wall. He grabbed his copy of *Bruce and Buddha: How Rock and Roll and Ancient Wisdom can be your Guide*, flipping quickly to dog-eared pages and searching for the yellow highlighted passages. He quickly skimmed from paragraph to paragraph, focusing exclusively on Michael's words, ignoring the blue and pink colors used to accentuate the words of others.

One of the great dangers of life is allowing past resentments to hold too much power over the present. Love can be hidden by the clouds of smoldering hostility. Why do we give such events so much authority in our lives? When past pain can veto current joy, life becomes more burden than blessing.

There is peril when thought patterns threaten to permanently cast you in the role of victim. It is a dangerous habit, this inclination to grant unnatural long life to your suffering, because you tend it like it were some prized flowerbed.

*Wishing the event had never happened will do nothing positive for you. You **cannot** wish away the past. Acceptance of this fact must occur in our deepest being, not just our intellect.*

Real strength is the ability to recognize your life is yours despite heartbreak and tragedy.

Father Sylvan closed the book and somberly returned it to the bookcase. He rubbed his chin, wondering what Michael Tanner had endured.

*The Master said: "That I've become a sage and mastered
Humanity? How could I say that of myself? I work
at it and teach it, never tiring. You could say that
much. But no more."*
-Confucius, *The Analects*, chapter 7.34

*We use these figures as they are always used by a culture; to
inspire ordinary lives by displaying their own potentialities.
Extraordinary people excite; they guide; they warn; standing,
as they do, in the corridors of imagination...they help
us carry what comes to us as it came to them.*
-James Hillman, *The Soul's Code*

CHAPTER 12
FUTURE VISIONS

"Okay, okay, okay," Michael groaned, clearly exasperated with the conversation looping to nowhere. Pushing his fingers through his thick, graying hair, he stood and scraped his chair along the floor. He released a deep sigh and circled the table where Brian, Melissa, and Reggie, a member of the marketing department at Idea Publishing, sat. They appeared to be at least as annoyed as Michael.

"This is just the way it has to be, Michael. It's the world you're in now." Melissa hoped her voice was instructive and not patronizing. Some hopes are stillborn.

No shit. "I understand that, Melissa. I do."

"Then why are you opposed to extending the tour after the weekend retreat?" Reggie asked plaintively. "There are plenty of venues we can schedule to keep your name active. While we do that, we plan some dates in England and Ireland, including a re-treat-style presentation or two. Our sister company in London reports there is real interest over there that we can tap into."

Michael looked at Brian, telepathically speaking to his longtime agent. *Has he listened to a fucking word I've said?*

"Reggie," Brian enunciated, one palm on his forehead as he strained to find the common ground, "it's not that Michael doesn't get what you're saying or the importance of continuing the marketing efforts."

"Hell," Michael interjected, "I'm even enjoying them."

"Then what is it?" Reggie asked. "Because all I feel sitting here is resistance."

Michael returned his chair to the table and sat. "It's not the tour."

"It's not the idea of going to Europe," added Brian.

"Shit, no," Michael confirmed. "That sounds great."

"Then what?" Melissa demanded, a pen in her hand despite the fact she hadn't taken a note for a good ten minutes.

"It's how you two are talking about the tour. About me." Michael leaned back from the table as if recoiling from something rancid. He drew a breath and brought himself back to the table, hands moving to accentuate his words and accusations. "I am not, nor do I want to be presented like, some self-help guru or keeper of secret knowledge that I have somehow been gifted with."

"But you kinda are that person," Reggie offered, thinking it was a compliment. "Even if you don't see it."

"No," Michael snapped. "That is not me."

"Fine. Then what are you?" Reggie pressed.

Michael shook his head and looked at Brian, who sighed and rubbed his head with both hands. After a few precious seconds slipped away, Brian answered on his client's behalf. "He's a corridor."

"He's a corridor?" Melissa asked. "What does that even mean?"

It means I'm empty. Nothing. "A corridor," Michael repeated, stretching himself to his full height. Melissa's eyes widened at the sight because Michael often walked with a scholar's stoop, his back permanently bent. Brian often mocked Michael for his hunched standing position, accusing him of attempting to downplay his height so as not to stand out or intimidate. "I've studied. I've lived. I've learned. I bring ideas from a variety of places to my readers. To audience members. But whatever, I don't know, wisdom they think they hear, whatever aid comes to them, whatever enthusiasm or inspiration they feel, well, none of it is me. Don't you see that?" *I am nothing.* "I'm just the corridor allowing these ideas passage to them and them passage to the ideas. I'm no guru. Not some great teacher. I am the corridor for people to traverse and, inevitably, forget."

"And that's how we are supposed to market you? As a corridor?" Reggie asked. "I don't think that'll work very well."

"We've gotten this far without building me up into some kind of commodity," Michael retorted. "Why can't it?"

Melissa delivered a blunt reply. "Because you're reaching a new strata. The special event we have planned, the overseas dates, even the success of this speaking tour have propelled you beyond where you started. That's always the goal. You have to keep up with these changes if you want this success to continue ."

"Do I?" Michael asked. *Is that some immutable, universal law?* "Let's say I recognize the need for promotions, because I do. You're telling me you can't find a way to publicize without making me appear to be some self-absorbed, self-help person? Do better. I am fine with my readers remembering the lessons and forgetting the teacher."

"Being forgotten isn't the way to maintain your new-found career," Melissa stated. Or spat, depending on how one interpreted her tone.

"He won't be," Brian assured. "That's not how people are. The point is we can promote the works without building up an image of Michael that he is not comfortable with and, frankly, he can't fulfill. We just need to be a little more creative."

"Or honest," Michael said, returning to his seat at the table. "Can't we just honor and seek truth?" *Why is that so hard?*

An almost comfortable silence extended for a few hour-long seconds while the foursome stewed. Reggie, in a trance and chasing an elusive thought, broke the silence. "That corridor thing just might work."

"How so?" Melissa asked. There was a tinge of hope in her voice.

"Picture this," Reggie posited as he stood up. "In the bigger presentations, we would have a large screen behind Michael. In front of the screen, we could actually build a large, maybe rounded, corridor. Have it touching the screen. The inner part of the rounded corridor should be a screen as well. We project the rest of that corridor onto the screen, receding back, back, like into time. While he speaks, images emerge from the screen, coming forward, eventually transferring from the screen to the inside of the corridor Michael presents from. He could almost be like a, um, a tour guide! Walking people through this wormhole. Walking us through time to help people encounter these ageless lessons and ideas! I'm just spitballing here, but what do you think? Have some potential?"

"Sounds a little, I don't know...," Melissa paused, searching for the correct words.

"Dorky?" Michael gave a weak smile as he was aware, and mildly annoyed, that there was a real possibility he and Melissa might be on the same page.

Melissa confirmed Michael's suspicion. "Yes, but it works for you. Not for many others I can think of but definitely for you. I mean that in a good way."

Michael snorted and shook his head. "I know. And I agree."

"Soooo, we want to make this corridor idea part of your future presentations?" Reggie asked tentatively.

"Not too big? Too showy?" Michael asked.

Brian patted Michael on the shoulder. "I see your concern. We could always quaint up the stage with some book shelves. Create a little library motif. The nice thing about that corridor is it would help drive home lessons. It would make them the focal point."

"And not me," Michael added quickly. "Imagine people leaving a room talking about Confucius, Buddha, and Bruce. That I like. I like that a lot."

"And they will." Brian was relieved to see the tension leaving his author's body. "Don't forget: this presentation is for larger venues, as opposed to your quainter town hall type setups that you can continue to have as well."

"Will continue to have," Melissa corrected kindly. "That's the backbone of this promotional tour. I know that. I just want something that we go to every once in a while, so we can bring in larger audiences while we have the interest to do it."

Michael hesitated, doubt infiltrating his thoughts. "Just one thing. All those visuals. Won't they be too distracting?"

Reggie held his hands up like he was directing traffic. "Hold on. Let's just slow down. This doesn't have to be the final setup or anything. I just feel like we have an idea of what Michael is and isn't comfortable with, and we know the goals we have for the ongoing promotion of the book. We have time to plan the presentation and decide the design of the stage. Michael, we are obviously going to want your input for us to plan the stage and images around your preferences."

"What about the weekend retreat?" Michael asked. "Should we be looking to use this format there?"

Brian responded, shaking his head. "We have put quite a bit of work into that presentation already. Don't think we want to shift gears now."

"Yeah," Michael agreed, "you're right. It would be much better to stick with what we've planned while looking to the future."

"Sounds good," Brian said. "Melissa? Reggie?"

Melissa took the initiative to speak for Reggie. "Yes. I'm feeling quite confident. Reggie and I will stay here to go over some of our notes and gauge what we need. See what's feasible and what's not. We'll touch base with you regarding our progress in a couple days."

Brian stood up and shook hands with Melissa and Reggie before exiting the room. "Excellent." Michael did the same and followed Brian.

The door was barely closed behind them when Brian spoke. "That went well. Glad you're on board."

"Always on board, boss. Just not always in agreement with what I hear."

"This I know and have known for a long time," Brian playfully groused.

They passed a few more doors and entered Brian's suite. Without asking Michael if he wanted one, he poured two glasses of Bushmills Whiskey. He held a glass aloft until it was taken from his hand. It was not a long wait.

"Why thank you, sir," Michael said.

"No problem. To moving forward."

"Moving forward," Michael repeated. He took a sip of his whiskey and sat in a plush chair, an easy smile on his face. "It is a bit amazing this is happening."

"It can feel that way. But it is very rewarding."

Michael answered with a nod of his head and the tilt of his glass. He settled into his chair, unaware of the clouds gathering on Brian's face. His longtime agent sighed and spoke, hoping he wasn't making a mistake. "Michael, we've been together a long time."

"Yes," Michael responded with a guarded tone. "We have."

"And in that time, we've acted like friends to each other."

"I would say we've become friends. I mean, I talked to you about my divorce, and you shared serious concerns with me after your son's car accident."

Brian raised a finger as if an unexpected idea had just leapt into his head. "Exactly! So, as a friend, I wanted to ask you something. It's just, um, I've seen how you look at Sara."

"Excuse me?"

"Sara. I see how you look at her. I can tell you're interested. I've known you fifteen years and have never seen you look at someone that way."

Michael scrutinized Brian's face, choosing what words he wanted to use quite carefully. "And you feel a need to tell me this because?"

"Be careful."

"Be careful? Of what? I am not even sure what I'm feeling because it's been so damn long since I've felt this way, and you tell me to be careful. What? Is she some kind of psychopath, and I am unaware?"

"No, I think—"

"Are you afraid it could cause us professional problems?"

"No. I mean, nothing that couldn't be worked out."

"Are you aware that whatever the hell I'm feeling is likely none of your business?"

"I know. I also know you. I know I saw you two laughing at the book launch a while back and looking very comfortable at the launching event for this tour. You two smile around each other a lot. It actually looks nice."

Michael sipped his drink and placed it somewhat heavily on the end table. "We look nice together so I should be careful. Could you make some fuckin' sense, please?"

"Listen. Sara's awesome. Great worker and a nice person. But in relationships? She's not too serious. Well, that's not quite it. She's reluctant to, y'know, unless, well, and if it gets, or even feels serious, she's out. Not sure you need that aggravation."

"Wow. Thanks for clarifying. That was helpful." Michael held up his glass and offered a droll toast to Brian. Smirking, Brian tapped his glass against Michael's. "As for aggravation. Aggravation? I'm not even sure what I'm feeling and, on a somewhat regular basis, I'm actually trying to talk myself out of feeling anything. And you're telling me she's the difficult one?"

"You know what I'm saying," Brian said. "You are a dedicated person who pours himself into things. You shouldn't be chasing a feather in the wind. You can't grab it. If you do, you can't keep it."

"First off, I get the feeling you're actually trying to look out for me here. Granted, in a bumbling kind of way, but still looking out, so that's nice of you. Secondly, I'll decide what I want to do and what chances I want to take, thank you. Thirdly, did you just give me a warning by quoting Led Zeppelin?"

"No! I was—no, definitely not."

"Because, while a feather in the wind is a common phrase, they did use it in "'All my Love.'"

"Oh. Yeah, that wasn't it." For unclear reasons, Brian looked uncertain in his own skin.

"Cool. Just—"

"Forrest Gump," Brian interrupted sheepishly. "I was thinking of the scene, you know, the feather drifting by, and he's sharing some wisdom from his momma. That's where it came from."

Michael stared at Brian for a moment before infectious laughter rose from his heart. "Holy shit, I can't believe you did that," teased Michael when his glee subsided.

Brian wiped laughter-induced tears from his eyes. "I know. It doesn't change that I think she is that way. Which is decidedly not your way. She can't give you what you need."

But she, without realizing it, already has. "I hear what you're saying, Brian. I do."

"That's good," Brian said. "And, hey, do what you will. I just wanted to say something. I've known you a long time is all. She is great! I just wanted to say something."

"I got it. No worries."

The two men touched glasses again and sipped their whiskey. Michael rested his head on the back of the chair for a few seconds. He closed his eyes and peacefully rolled his head so he was facing Brian. His eyes shot open, as a thought flashed in his mind. "Wait a minute. Are you comparing me to Forrest Gump because he fumbles through life and is hopelessly devoted to the wrong woman?"

"What? No!" Brian ceased his defense when he saw Michael flash an impish grin. "You're such an ass."

"Maybe," Michael allowed in a dismissive tone accompanied by a Cheshire grin.

"Maybe? Trust me, it's a sure thing."

"I see. Well, whatever the future holds for this ass, I guarantee you one thing."

"What's that?"

"I'll fight the good fight—"

"—with all thy might."

It is spiritless to think that you cannot attain
to that which you have seen and heard the
masters attain. The masters are men. You are also a man.
If you think that you will be inferior in doing
something,
you will be on that road very soon.
-Yamamoto Tsunetomo, *Hagakure*
(Translator William Scott Wilson)

CHAPTER 13
FACING A DEMON

11:30. Michael sighed as he sat in bed. His pen moved across a page of his journal, ideas for future books taking shape on the blank paper. An hour had passed since he started writing. He thought about attempting to go to sleep but was discouraged by the idea of not sleeping. *Great. Now I can't sleep because I'm anxious about going to sleep. Fuck.*

Unfortunately, writing was now no longer productive because fatigue was sapping his concentration and creativity. His eyes closed, and he let his mind drift for a moment, allowing himself to feel tired. Just settling into his pillow, his cell phone buzzed. A smile appeared on his face when he saw Sara's name.

Hey. Just saw your message and wanted to answer. Thanks for checking in. Bedtime was a challenge, as always. Hopefully you're already resting.

Hey, Sara. I am just turning in. I feel your pain. Bedtime with my
youngest was always an adventure.
Oh! Sorry to bother you. Get some sleep.

No bother. I was writing. Enjoying time away?
Absolutely. Not that the tour isn't exciting. You know what I'm saying.
I do. Family is important. See you in a couple days?
Yup. I'm turning in. Good night.
Good night. Sleep well.
Thanks. You as well! Have a good day tomorrow. You deserve it!

Michael put down his phone with a contented sigh. *Good night, Sara* was his last thought before sleep overtook him.

***

Michael stood in the dilapidated gym where the creature had delivered his previous beating. Where the creature always began the beatings. The room was exactly the same. No. There was a locker, three lockers, along the side wall. Dumbbells of various weights were on the floor. Dust and cobwebs were all that tried to lift them.

Where was the creature? Michael sensed its presence. Its unrelenting fury drifted like an invisible mist in the air, creating a free-floating anxiety that could not be ignored. But it could not be heard. Where was it? Heart pounding, Michael looked around the room. *What to do? Hide in a locker? No. That would not do. Head to the street? Hide under the boxing ring?* It seemed pointless. Hopeless. *What to do?*

A guttural snarl came from the street, followed by the shrieks of wraiths fleeing to ensure their ghastly existence. *No. Nononono. Not ready. What to do? Wait. The dumbbells. Could they be used to hurt the creature? Stun it and escape into the street? Find somewhere else to be? Maybe. Maybe.*

Michael collected weights that he could lift with ease. Scanning the room again, he formed a plan to place dumbbells in the ring and slide underneath its frame to the corner farthest from the street. Now wait. Just wait and hope? Had he earned the right to hope?

Wood flew and the building shook—*how could something so fearsome move so fast?*—when the creature crashed its way into the gym. A roar was cut short and replaced by a snort. Then another while the creature looked for its prey. The lockers fell victim to the beast's ire as holes were punched through the rusty metal. Snarling, frustrated, the beast approached the boxing ring. The floor cringed under increasingly thunderous footfalls. A wrathful growl was the precursor to a fist smashing through the boxing ring and the floor below. The dirt and rock of the creature's arm were stuck in the floor for a moment, and this was when Michael emerged from hiding.

Michael leapt into the boxing ring and lifted two five-pound weights, throwing them into the creature's face, which was about level with him. The monster stood in the ring, bent over, arm still stuck in the floor. Michael lifted a twenty-five-pound dumbbell and charged across the ring, bringing the weight crashing down once, then twice, on the creature's head. It bellowed and stood upright. How Michael wished the sounds emanating from the beast communicated pain. They did not. Michael's attack was no more than the rain falling into the ocean. *Fuck! Do you even feel pain?*

A massive fist grabbed Michael and sent him hurtling across the room. The wall barely held its ground when the projectile that was Michael collided against it. A pained groan exited Michael's soul when he fell to the floor. For reasons he didn't understand, Michael stood and faced the beast, his back pressed against the cracked wood and plaster. He stepped to his side toward the gaping hole that led to a corridor. Four more steps and he could dash from the room. Flee the horror before him. One step was all that the creature allowed.

A sharpened vine flew from the creature's palm, impaling Michael while simultaneously keeping him upright. The creature raised its arm, and Michael was hoisted some four feet off the floor. Two more vines flew, piercing his right shoulder and left thigh. Michael screamed. The beast howled.

Was the foul thing joyful? There seemed to be a subtle elation hidden in the bellows of the beast, the rapture of having found its prey. Such a sound was only further insult to Michael, and he grimaced and groaned on the end of the three vines, blood pooling below him. *Why must you wound me so? Is there no mercy in you?* Such foolish questions, for there was no sympathy in the abyss. Michael's attention turned from the creature to the hands that gripped the ensnarling vines. *What is this wood that kills me? Is it ash? I am not Odin consecrated to myself on the world tree. There is no hard-won wisdom to be found here. No gifts of foresight granted in nine days. Only pain. These vines are not cedar, pine, and cyprus. There is no victory here. Only defeat. Only defeat.*

Michael writhed on the vines and panted for breath at the end of his gruesome leash. Saplings sprouted from the vines and inched their way down Michael's arms and up his legs. The wood burrowed into his body, digging through flesh and muscle. Wrapped around

Michael's forehead, the spreading vines held his head still. They forced him to stare at his torturer. The vines, at the bidding of their master, carried him back to the boxing ring. He was dropped to the floor and pummeled by rock-encrusted fists. One, two, three blows and finally, almost mercifully, thrown through a window to land in a heap on the street. A few seconds free of vicious attention. A few precious seconds.

Somehow Michael rose to his feet. What stupidity. No longer seeking a battle plan, his desire was not to be crushed to the earth any longer. He sought to flee. An alley was visible some fifty yards away. Perhaps refuge was there. Michael staggered, chasing the mirage of hope. Turning the corner, he saw a strip of pavement strewn with paper and trash. Paper plates. Uneaten food. Diapers. Old clothes. The remnants of lost life and disposable years. Michael stumbled down the alley, a trail of blood behind him. Despairing he was merely delaying his demise, he tumbled into a dumpster about halfway down the alley and pulled the garbage stored within over his body.

The beast entered the alley and howled, announcing the arrival of death. It lumbered to the dumpster. Blood stained the receptacle. Michael peered from beneath the garbage, settling deeper into the refuse. Through the cracks in the lid, the creature could be seen sniffing the air. It looked at the dumpster and stretched its arms, grabbing either end of the metal container. With a wretched snarl, the dumpster was ripped in half, garbage falling to the ground while other scraps were tossed into the air. The creature searched the pile. His prey could not be found. Deprived of its plaything, the creature hurled the metal scraps of the dumpster out of the alley. A shriek born of rage and frustration shook neighboring buildings. Michael had dissipated into the trash. The very essence of his body and being became one with each piece of paper. Every rotten core. All the stained napkins were Michael. He had escaped the beast by becoming trash. By becoming waste. By becoming something easily discarded and ignored. Unwanted. Unneeded.

***

A scream escaped from Michael as he shot up in his bed. *Garbage. Waste. Unwanted. What? Where? Calm yourself. Calm yourself. What was that? I'm garbage? No. Yes.* He rose from the bed and allowed trembling legs to carry him to the window. He barely made it. A knot in his stomach tightened, causing him to gasp for breath. *I'm garbage? No. No. Yes.* It was three in the morning, and the night sky was clear. Stars sparkled and a bright moon shone. It should have been a beautiful sight, but Michael noticed it not at all. Sleep was done, beauty was dead, and the nightmare loomed; a grim specter haunted the room. It was different this time, but better? How could this be better? The only escape was through becoming filth? *I'm garbage.* He rubbed his face and went to his nightstand, pawing the surface until he found his cell. Some quick motions of his fingers and Sara's last message glowed on the screen before him.

You deserve it!

I'm garbage? No. Yes. Yes, I am. A lone tear fell and rolled over Sara's name. He descended to the floor and cried alone, a moonbeam his only companion. *Garbage.* With his waning energy, he tossed his cell phone aside. Where it landed was of no consequence. All that mattered was that he, at the very least, could protect Sara's name from his pain. Sometimes a river of tears is best unleashed alone.

CHAPTER 14
SEEKING CALMER WATERS

Just a reminder that I will be on campus today. Still meeting you and Barry for dinner afterwards?

The instant the message was sent, a knot formed in Michael's stomach, completely disproportionate to the simple message. He anticipated the response like a child awaiting Christmas morning. It would be good, very good, to see old friends right now. Especially Carol and Barry Wilson. Michael and Carol worked together for years in the English Department at Roaring River University. The two had forged a deep friendship, helping each other with professional frustrations and personal hurdles. Michael considered the lack of contact with Carol one of the few aspects of his previous life that he missed. He was thankful that distance, and their now distinct paths, had not weakened their connection. It was through Carol that Michael befriended Barry, her husband. The two men had become so close that Carol playfully accused her husband of "stealing" her friend.

That evening, Michael was returning to Roaring River to discuss writing, publishing, and whatever else the Young Writer's Society wished to discuss. Prior to the meeting with the students, he would be a guest lecturer in ENG207: Writing Creative Nonfiction, followed by what he hoped would be a brief sit-down with members of the administration. Thankfully, the session with the Young Writer's Society was on the schedule, creating a definite deadline for the meeting with the school administrators. Michael could tolerate only so many self-aggrandizing comments pitifully disguised as sincere compliments. Following his discussion with the Young Writer's Society would be a signing at a local bookstore. Even without the recent rash of nightmares or the minor stressor of returning to the campus, dinner with Carol and Barry would be most welcome. Getting to that engagement would be the challenge.

Michael focused on the previous night, pulling his mind away from his looming schedule. Tears. Tears had fallen, poured from his eyes, and Michael was disturbed by this. How near the edge was he? *Garbage.* Why were his emotions this raw? *Waste.* What dam was cracking? *Unwanted.* He had an idea but also knew initial inklings were rarely correct. The loosening of one knot, he had learned, meant little more than sliding down the rope, only to encounter another. It was the end of the strand, not the middle, which held his thoughts captive. He knew nothing would be resolved sitting in his hotel room. Another morning walk was in order.

Three laps around the park brought a sense of relief, though not as much as the message from Carol. Dinner at a local steak house was confirmed. *Thank God. It will be good to see them.* What to do in the interim remained a question. Michael carried his journal but did not feel inclined to write. Instead he sat on a bench by the pond to see if he could get something out of doing nothing. A garbage can to his left was close to overflowing, some paper lying in the grass next to it. He stood and cleaned the area, pushing the mound of waste deeper into the receptacle. Something in his stomach turned to stone as he did so.

Surprised by the sudden discomfort, Michael returned to the bench and drew a few quick breaths into his abdomen. A longer, slower breath followed and then another. The knot in his stomach loosened. He tried to slip into a meditative state, eyes closed and the gentle warmth of the sun on his face. Thoughts drifted into his consciousness. Some he successfully allowed to float by like clouds across the spacious sky of his mind. But quickly, fiercer images arose. His mind grasped at them, held them tight even as he tried to calm his nerves. Whatever peace he sought was lost while unexpected images invaded his thoughts.

Black, pressed pants with a sharp crease descended a flight of stairs. This sight wrenched his mind momentarily before giving way to the beast from his dream. Immovable. Unflinching. A relentless horror of dirt and rock emerging, once again, from his subconscious with no purpose but to terrorize. Dirt and rock. Then a cascade of images ran a frantic race across his mind, ratcheting his anxiety. Hands sculpted clay. A voice whispered, "Go away and get cured," taunting his powerlessness. His stomach tightened. The simple act of sitting still became impossible. Michael opened his eyes. *Get a grip. Calm yourself.*

An audible grunt escaped Michael's lips when he stood up. Irritated, he strode away from the bench. Looking around the park, he contemplated another lap or two but thought a new path needed to be trod. He pulled his cell phone from his pocket and hit the number two. The third ring was interrupted by a young woman's voice.

"Hi, Dad. What's up?"

"Hey, Lu-lu! How do you do?" Much to Michael's amusement, he heard Lucy giggle at his time-honored greeting. "That one still gets you."

Lucy Tanner attempted a deadpan tone in reply. She failed quite miserably. "Yeah, Dad. You're a riot."

"I know. So, how's my favorite oldest daughter? How are classes?"

Lucy sighed, and she ignored the first question and focused on her academics. "Not bad. I mean, it's early in the semester, but they are going alright. How's the book tour? Exciting?"

"Very." Michael was pleased with the feeling of authentic enthusiasm that gripped his voice. "We are in a planned lull right now, but we will be getting busier starting tonight."

"Cool. Another presentation?"

"Nope. Visiting Roaring River. Then a book signing."

"Got it."

"Talk to your mother lately?"

"Well, maybe."

"Hey. Call your mother. She'll appreciate it. Come to think of it, call me more often. I would appreciate it. Ever since you turned twenty-one and started getting serious with Brett, you've done a terrible job keeping in touch," Michael half-joked.

"That's it," Lucy teased her father. "Nothing to do with the fact that this is my senior year, and I'm trying to wrap my mind around my requirements, a major thesis, a community project, and applications to graduate school."

Michael pretended to be unimpressed by his daughter's busy schedule. "That's my point exactly. You have plenty of free time to call your old man."

"Okay," Lucy lightly laughed.

"Seriously now, how's all that going?"

"Good, actually." Lucy sounded confident, although Michael heard the concealed trepidation in her voice. "I have excellent partners and a productive study group that is really helpful."

"And Brett?"

"What about him?"

"Still treats you nice?"

"All the time. And he understands my workload and gives me the space I need."

Michael could picture his daughter's smile as she discussed her boyfriend. "That's good. Sounds like you've got everything under control."

"I have a semisolid grip on things," Lucy said. This time her voice was filled with trepidation tinged with a hint of concealed confidence.

"For argument's sake, I'll say I believe you."

"Thanks, Dad."

"No problem. Inspiration is what I'm here for. Speaking of inspiration, I haven't had a chance to share my brilliance with your younger sister lately. Have you spoken to Mary at all?"

"Nope. She can be tough to get a hold of. Well, not talking like—"

"Like us old people who actually speak into our phones still?" Michael broke in.

"Exactly! We text quite a bit though."

Michael nodded, pleased that the sisters were staying in contact. "That's good. She's a bit different than you. I'm not always sure—"

"Don't worry," Lucy interrupted. "She's doing fine in college."

"Yeah, well, I liked it better when she was homesick the first two weeks. Then she would respond to my messages. Now that's she's settled, she may as well be on Mars."

"She's doing fine. Besides, she has a good dad. I'm sure that counts for something when sending a kid to college."

"Thank you, Lucy. Need some money?"

"I'm doing okay. Why do you ask?"

"Well," Michael smiled, "that was quite a compliment. I assumed you were buttering me up."

Lucy groaned. "Geeeez. I don't remember a chapter in your book about the virtue of cynicism. Guess I'll have to reread it."

"I'm planning my next book," Michael said. "I think the title will be *Forgotten Fathers: The Pitfalls of Raising Independent Girls.*"

"Nice title. So, therapy is going well, I see," Lucy's delighted tone made the final words of the sentence barely audible.

"Why yes, it is," Michael declared proudly. "I'm going to let you go, Luce. If I'm not mistaken, you have a class soon, correct?"

"Yes, I do," Lucy confirmed. "I'm walking across campus now."

"Sounds good. Enjoy your day, Luce. I love you."

"I love you too, Dad. I will call you before Thanksgiving."

"Alright. Guess that means I will call you before you call me."

"Probably."

"Bye, Luce"

"Bye, Dad."

Michael had barely ended the call when a text from Lucy came in.

But I will text you before you call! Love you

Michael beamed at the message even while he wondered how his daughter typed that fast. The fact she used her thumbs and he pecked along with his index finger may have had something to do with unraveling this puzzle. He took a deep breath, pleased to discover his stomach was loosened. He also knew this was a respite from the growing current of anxiety. Fatigue was weakening the fortress of his mind. Troubled tides would only continue to rise if he could not find a way to permanently buttress his walls.

Ponder for a long time whether you shall admit a given person to your friendship; but when you have decided to admit him, welcome him with all your heart and soul. Speak as boldly with him as with yourself.
-Seneca, *Moral Letters to Lucilius* (Letter 3)

CHAPTER 15
OLD FRIENDS

Chuck's Chop Block was a great choice for dinner. The food was always impeccable, particularly the whiskey marinated steaks that Michael had come to love during his tenure at Roaring River. The no-frills menu may have seemed simple to certain eyes but no matter what you ordered, be it pork chops or fried seafood, you had yourself a true treat. The service was still outstanding, and the slightly dimmed dining room added to an atmosphere of comfortable intimacy. Chuck's was a true gem.

Despite his affinity for Chuck's, Michael would have been just as happy eating an old shoe in a cave, provided Carol and Barry were present. Their company was most welcome—Michael found himself more relaxed than he had felt in some time. Dinner was over, and somehow dessert, miraculously, found a home in the evening. The three friends now sat at a table with another round of drinks in hand. Michael enjoyed a McClelland's single malt scotch on the rocks. Whether it was his third or fourth was unknown. Barry was working on another Guinness, the drink Michael started the evening with before moving on. Carol held a glass of Caymus cabernet.

The friends settled their bill with their server and moved to a small table in the lounge area. Carol had just sat in her chair when she hesitantly, but most happily, posed a question to Michael. "So, who is she?"

"Excuse me?" Michael responded. "I thought we covered this during dinner. Happily single. No prospects. Don't want any."

"Avoiding romantic attachments like the plague," Barry added, rubbing Michael's neck. "Good for you." One of the joys of Barry was that occasionally his deadpan humor made it impossible to discern if he was joking or not and, if he was joking, who or what was being mocked. Michael spared a quick glance at Barry as he sought to interpret the comment. Barry, for his part, simply tipped his glass to Carol. "Carry on, my love."

Deciding he had been insulted, Michael unleashed some brotherly venom on Barry. "You know what? I am going to punch you in the throat later. Better watch your back."

"Technically my throat is in the front."

"You know what I mean, asshole." Satisfied with the gravity of his threat, Michael turned his attention to Carol. "Do carry on, 'my love.'"

"Hey," Barry snapped, "she's my love!"

Michael wore a devious smile on his face. "Don't be so sure. You know I know things. The ice under your feet might be thinner than you think."

"Oh, it's on! Later this evening, sir, we will settle this like men!"

"Wing eating contest?"

"You're on!"

Carol loosed a sigh that halted the men's banter. "Are you two done?"

Barry lifted his beer, saluting his wife.

Michael rolled his eyes with playful disdain. "You're such a kept man." His attention turned to Carol. "For your second question, I think I prefer the banter to the conversation you're trying to foist upon me."

Carol smirked while she gauged Michael's actual discomfort with the topic against his willingness to engage. "It's a simple question, really. So, who is she?"

"There's no one," Michael repeated.

"That's not what your face revealed," Carol replied.

"I don't know," Barry interjected. "He looks pretty serious."

"During dinner, dear." Carol reached out and patted her husband's face.

"I don't have an 'I'm interested in somebody but trying to hide it' face," Michael protested.

Barry nodded his head and grabbed Michael's arm. "I don't think he has that face either."

"Thanks. Your support is so greatly appreciated," Michael deadpanned.

"See? I have my own thoughts."

"You're a tower of resolve."

"Oh, sweetie," Carol cooed, "your thought is quite wrong. You should have stuck with me. And while it is true, Michael, that you don't have an 'I'm interested blah, blah, blah' face, you do have an 'I am so pumped up about this new book idea that I'm going to burst' face."

Barry conceded. "You do have that face. I've seen it."

"And you wore it tonight, right after I initially asked if you were seeing anyone."

"I didn't catch that," Barry admitted.

"Well, to be fair, you did a nice job trying to hide it, Michael. It was brief, but I saw it. It may as well have been in neon lights. You can deny it. Just know, I won't believe you. We can change topics, but I know you're lying to me."

Michael stared across the table into Carol's powerful brown eyes. Whatever form of silent communication the two had developed over the years was on full display; words and thoughts flowed from one friend's eyes to the other's. "Fine," Michael relented, leaning back and taking a sip of his scotch. His mood lightened as a smile blazed a path on his face. "There is someone I am, god, just astoundingly interested in."

Carol let go a fist pump. "Yes! I knew it! That's great!"

"Really?" Barry asked. "It is great, but, damn."

"Yes, dear, you were wrong again. Seventeen years and you still haven't learned." Content with having mocked her husband, Carol focused on Michael. "You haven't asked her out yet, correct?"

"Nope," Michael blurted. "I am still wrapping my mind around feeling this way. It's been a long time since I've felt like this. A very long time."

"That's really awesome! I mean it. You sometimes work too hard at keeping that part of life away from you that, well, that's awesome!" Barry exclaimed to Michael's surprise.

Carol nodded in agreement. "It is, but I don't understand. What do you mean 'a long time'? You've been attracted to people since your divorce. I mean, you've felt this way since then."

"No," Michael replied, shaking his head, "I haven't. I mean, yes, I've asked women out on dates, but this is different."

"How?" Carol asked.

Michael thought for a second before replying. "Remember when I approached Julia right after I was just divorced? I was walking around on trembling earth, not feeling solid."

"You were a bit off but not that bad," Carol shared. "Well, at least not if my memory serves me well."

"Of course," Michael said. "I mean, it's not like the turmoil I hide is ever any greater than what I show."

Carol laughed heartily. She occasionally wondered if she should take such delight in Michael's self-deprecating humor. This was not one of those times. "Okay. I believe you. You were a mess"

"That's more like it." Michael pointed a finger at Carol. "I was a mess! Well, maybe not a complete mess, but I was—"

"Michael," Carol said like a mother trying to garner a child's attention. "Yes?"

"Stop thinking so much and just speak."

"Okay. Anyway, she did us both a favor by saying no. I just didn't want to—or maybe didn't know how to—be alone. I don't know if she knew she was dodging a bullet at the time, but goddamn, she did."

"Hey!" Barry exclaimed, an impish grin appearing on his face. "Remember there was that woman you sorta dated for about a month?"

"Oh, Stacey," Michael confirmed, not attempting to cover his embarrassment.

"That was hilarious! You asked her out, I swear, to stay in practice approaching people. You were so fuckin' shocked she said yes. Then she had a great time with you, and you ended up going on two other dates because you felt guilty that she enjoyed your company. You didn't know how to let her down. That was awful."

"Yeah," Michael grimaced, "you sound real choked up about it."

"But you were legitimately attracted to that woman Marcy, even though you never actually approached her," Carol noted, a mild reprimand laced in her words.

Michael looked at Carol, silently communicating he heard her telepathic message and wished he could rebuke it. "No, I did not. I was attracted to her. I definitely was."

"And honestly," Barry interjected, "she was probably the best overall match for you at that stage of your life."

"Probably, but I never saw anything from her that made me think she was interested, so I never put real effort into it. I just let the thought of her go. That was never like this."

"How so?" Carol asked.

"This new woman, Sara, she lingers in my thoughts, despite the fact I wish she didn't. That somehow, when I awake from what limited sleep I get, she is usually already on my mind before my feet hit the floor. I'm amazed I can feel this way at forty-five. I didn't think I could. Christ, it feels like she's already important to me. My life is becoming increasingly hectic, and I have no doubt at all that it's going to get even crazier. I also know I would find a way to carve out time for her. We haven't gone on a date and it doesn't matter. The minutes of her life that I am able to steal are precious. Jesus, Mary, and Joseph, listen to me, babbling like some love-struck fool. I might need an exorcism."

"You know what? Even if this doesn't work out, it is great you're letting yourself feel this way," Carol said. "It really is."

"Sounds like you've known her a while," Barry surmised.

"Top scores, brotha. Over a year," Michael confirmed. "She works for Brian. Every time I interacted with her, I was impressed. Initially it was her professional judgment, energy, and thoughtfulness. Then, as we got better acquainted, it was with her. She's a dirt chewer and, even though it would embarrass her to hear it, she handles it with a certain grace."

"Dirt chewers," Barry said, raising his drink. Glasses were brought together, and a whimsical smile appeared on Carol's face. She loved Michael's pet phrase for people who have extra challenges in life. People who have lived and been forcefully kicked in the teeth by life and mustered the strength to marshal on. "So she's one of us."

"Oh yeah," Michael confirmed. "Without a doubt. I don't know any great details, but there is no doubt."

"You are clearly into her," Barry noted. "Why haven't you asked her out yet? The whole work thing? That can be a complication."

Michael stared at some distant thought, considered its validity, and took a deep breath. "Nah. That's not it."

"Then what?" Carol asked.

"I don't think I should approach her unless I can open the Door."

"Open the—oh no, Michael. No." Carol's eyes pained at the prospect. "Why put that on yourself? I mean, you don't know if it's necessary."

"I don't know what she'll say, that's true. It is, however, necessary. For her."

"For her?" Barry asked. "Not to be rude, but she's not a part of that."

"Not directly, but as I said, she matters to me; she's important to me. I need to know that I am stronger, stronger than I think I am, so she's not burdened by it."

"I don't understand," Carol confessed. "You always told me that people in relationships don't need to completely get rid of their luggage. They just need to find the strength to, at times, let the other person carry it—"

Barry finished his wife's thought, taking her hand as he did so. "—While trusting that the other person is willing. You know how much those words helped us."

"I do."

"Then why not heed your advice and leave it be? If she says yes, and you two become something, then deal with it later."

"That's the point," Michael said. "That's the whole fucking thing. I was okay with that idea with the others. Of just easing things along. But for her, and my hopes, I need to walk through. I will still have shit to carry, but I must reduce the load. To look in a mirror and know I won't be walking a half mile behind and dragging her down like some anchor. I feel like I owe her that."

"Her?" Carol asked. "Just her?"

"Myself too. For the first time, I feel like I want to face this for someone, for her. Instead of asking someone to deal with it because they're with me. Or might be with me."

"You know, you're not the man you were when you approached Kate with this. And I'm not sure she was equipped to help you. To stand by your side. Please don't let that make you hesitate with Sara," Carol's voice pleaded as her eyes continued to send comfort and strength across the space between friends.

"Kate handled it the way she could. You being right in some regard doesn't mean I handled everything heroically. Marriages don't end because of the failures of one person. And, in the end, who cares? That's done," Michael emphasized. "Whatever remnants of that remains, I'll deal with. As for the present, I know I have to do this. I mean, the nightmares have returned."

"The nightmares?" Barry asked, confusion becoming realization in the single beat of the heart. "You mean the recurring nightmares you had when you first started to confront things? Even before you spoke of those things to Kate?"

"Yup. Haven't had them in years. They started up again."

"I think I am understanding your sense of urgency," Barry said quietly. "Same images?"

"Same ineffective resistance. Same beatings. Same powerlessness."

"Same inability to sleep?" Barry asked.

"Yup. Are we on the clock? Should I get my insurance card?"

"Never. Besides, you're a better armchair psychologist than most of the well-trained newbies in my office. You're sure the dream is exactly the same?"

"Pretty much. The beast. The Door. The gym. The street. It's all there. Oh, except the ending of my most recent dream—I hid. There was no death blow that woke me up."

"Really? Interesting change."

"Not really," Michael stated. "I turned into garbage at the end of the dream. That's how I escaped. Hundreds of worthless scraps of paper containing my consciousness drifting on the breeze and falling into puddles. It was awful."

"Doesn't sound pleasant, but it is a change. So you just ran and hid in the garbage?"

"No," Michael corrected. "I tried to fight. Got thrown around. Impaled. It was gruesome. Then I fled."

Barry bit his lower lip while he weighed the new information. His hand dropped on the table, rattling it slightly more than planned. "You've gotta open the Door."

"But now?" Carol asked Barry before turning her attention to Michael. "You've worked so hard. Your entire life, even. You've fought, fallen, and rose again. Why go there? Just see if she wants a cup of coffee with you."

"I don't know," Michael said. "To feel worthy, I suppose. A cup of coffee, lunch, or shopping for groceries—it doesn't matter. I want to stand before Sara and know I am not concealing my weaknesses out of fear. Actively being defensive with her. If the time comes to broach things, and I hope it does, I want to know I'm ready to be... strong? Not sure that's the right word. That I am not looking to her to be some kind of, I don't know, healer? That I'm...something. Sorry. I am not explaining this terribly well. I hope you have at least some understanding of why."

"I think I do," Barry said. "I'm not you, but I think I get it. Though I would like to say it's not just her. In fact, the hell with this new person. Seriously, she's a side thought at the moment. I know she seems important to you, but I do not see her as the cause of your nightmares returning."

"No?"

"Not at all. You have made improvements in life and dared to take chances. Now your life is expanding a bit beyond your control.

You're being noticed. Eyes are on you, and people are listening in numbers you never imagined. The idea, the need to feel worthy of their time, and I know you take that thought quite seriously, might be playing out in both the big and small stages of your life."

Michael nodded. He stared into his glass, pausing for a sigh before finishing the watered down contents. "There is often more than one motivator in the pie charts of our lives. Anyway, Sara comes back tomorrow. I can figure out what I'm going to do over the next few days. Maybe have it sorted through before we leave for San Diego."

"I just don't know how you do it," Carol said.

"Do what?"

"Your plunges into your dark places. I can't do it. Especially not like you do. I don't always get you, but I always root for you."

"Then regardless of what the future holds with Sara, I am blessed in my friendships."

"Well said!" Barry exclaimed. "To prove your sincerity, you should pay for my drinks tonight."

"Oh," Michael's face puckered like he had just eaten something sour, "this is awkward. I was only talking about Carol."

Laughter returned to the table, as did the server. She was not surprised to take an order for another round.

CHAPTER 16
THROUGH THE EYES OF FRIENDS

Carol and Barry giggled upon entering their comfortable home. The laughter was augmented by their shared discomfort with Uber, a feeling which sometimes conflicted with their shared appreciation for the service provided.

"Thank goodness we're home," Carol proclaimed. "God! I hate the fact that you can't have any real discussions when Ubering."

Barry smiled quizzically at his wife. "Ubering? Is that even a word?"

"Well, it is now! And you know what I mean!"

"I do indeed, my lady. But while we're at it, thank goodness for Uber because it enabled us both to have an extra drink."

"Or two."

"Or two!"

Carol raised her empty hand to toast and snickered, seeing Barry was in the same pose. "What do you think? One more?"

"Thought you'd never ask," Barry responded happily. "Want me to get it?"

Carol shook her head and waved him off. "Nah. Take a seat. I got it."

Barry sat on the living room couch as Carol swept into the kitchen. He had barely settled in when a question flew into the room.

"Wine or whiskey?"

"How do you know I don't want a beer?"

"You don't."

Barry sat in silence for a moment, weighing his craving for a drink against the desire to prove his wife wrong. His internal dilemma solved, he voiced his request. "Fine, you're right."

"I usually am," a victorious voice sang from the kitchen.

Barry loved the playful qualities his wife still possessed despite the passage of time. "I'm going with a glass of wine, my dear."

"Wine it is," Carol called back and placed the bottle of Glenlivet 12 back on the counter. "Must admit, didn't see that coming."

"I'm a renowned man of mystery," Barry called back through a smirk that only grew when Carol entered the room with an exaggerated, incredulous look on her face.

"Yeah," she groaned upon delivering his glass, "that's it."

"Well," Barry tapped his glass against hers, "I'm definitely something."

"That you are."

"Hey, I must be. Kept you around all these years."

"It's the money," Carol teased. "You're my sugar daddy." The couple laughed and shared a quick kiss before Carol turned the conversation elsewhere. "Speaking of couples—"

"Here we go," Barry snorted.

"What?"

"Time to discuss Michael and his affections for this, what was her name?"

"Sara. Don't you listen to people for a living?"

"Yeah, but I take notes."

"Touché." Carol reached out to touch glasses again before taking another sip of wine. "So, my dear, what are your thoughts on Michael and Sara?"

"Um, well, honestly, I hope she doesn't feel the same way."

"Really?" Barry asked, legitimately surprised. "But you told us at dinner you thought it was great he feels the way he does."

"Oh, I meant it. But he's not ready to actually be in a real relationship. He's still a touch too raw."

"Do tell, what brought you to that conclusion? But first," Barry said quickly before his wife could speak, "let us take a moment to acknowledge that I quoted something you mentioned at dinner. You see? Great. Listener."

"Or, perhaps, a great douchebag."

"There is that," Barry conceded. "Seriously, why the hopes for a brokenhearted Michael?"

"That's not exactly what I'm hoping for. He just, I think he is truly surprised that he feels this strongly for her. I'm just not sure it's her. I think he's just amazed he's actually allowing himself to be open to the idea of a relationship and this Sara is simply geographically convenient."

"Ouch. Aren't you the romantic? So, all these positive traits he mentioned—her energy, her thoughtfulness—that's all projections or, at the least, exaggerations?"

"I wouldn't go that far. I am sure he is not deluding himself that she has these traits. She might be wonderful. But better suited for him two years from now when his feet are even firmer on the ground. I just don't think he's quite ready for a relationship yet and, you know, he's not the casual type. He'll dive in with all he can."

"That's for sure," Barry said.

"But you disagree with the other points I made?"

"Not entirely. I mean, when I said the hell with this new person at dinner, I meant it. For the record, I do think you're right about his level of rawness. He would be an odd combination of tentative and enthusiastic in a relationship right now. I, however, could care less what she says as long as he goes for it. That's important for him right now. A yes. A no. So what? You work with what happens."

"If she says yes, he gets hurt in the long run. He's not ready yet."

"Who's ready?" Barry responded. "Every new relationship brings challenges, both foreseen and unexpected, to a person's life. He did call her a dirt chewer, so maybe she's not 'ready yet' either. And maybe they stumble along together and help each other find a fine road. Maybe they grow for a spell and split up, wiser and stronger for the experience. Maybe nothing happens. But one of Michael's traits is the ability to think himself into inaction. It would be nice to see him not do that."

"That's a very good point. You, Barry Wilson," Carol's fingers interlocked with her husband's, "can be quite a smart man."

Barry offered a gentle kiss before he spoke. "Why, thank you."

"So, to recap."

"By all means, Professor, what did we learn today?"

"That wine was the drink of choice on the couch tonight. That Michael is not actually ready for a relationship, but he should go for it."

"Don't forget we learned that I am smart and, by extension, a renowned man of mystery."

"Or, at the very least, a douchebag," Carol mocked and placed her head on his shoulder.

"There is that." Barry leaned his head onto hers. They sat in silence, their breathing reaching a harmonious rhythm while they enjoyed the quiet perfection of the moment. Perhaps, without realizing it, they sent a prayer forth that Michael's life would reverberate with such moments again as well.

CHAPTER 17
LENDING A HAND

Michael burst from his room with extra energy in his step. The unexpected afternoon nap he had just awoken from provided a welcome increase in energy. That, along with the enthusiasm he always felt when a presentation approached, explained the bouncing strides with which he attacked the hall. The elevator took him to the lobby. He planned to circle the park for a lap or two before grabbing a quick bite at Mary's. He promised Brian they would drive to the convention hall together, providing time to discuss travel plans and the expansion of the tour.

The sight of Sara making her way across the lobby changed his plans. She wore large sunglasses, dark enough to conceal her mystical eyes. Black hair fell haphazardly from beneath a bandana that was straining to stay on her head. Blue jeans and a red sweater all but completed her casual attire. A travel bag denied the laws of physics as it stayed draped over one shoulder despite what appeared to be an impossible angle. She shrugged her shoulders to maintain the bag while she dragged a rolling suitcase behind her. Her purposeful gait made it clear she did not want to be bothered. Sara made a beeline toward the lobby's café. Of course, the possibility did exist that she was merely attempting to keep pace with her latest collection of whirling thoughts.

"Sara!" Michael called from the elevator that he now held open with his left hand.

Her face lit up with recognition when she heard the sound of his voice. "Michael!" She veered over like she was engaged in a speed walking contest. "Excellent timing."

"Someone must be watching out for you. Were you going to get something to eat? I was just heading out."

"No. Honestly, I thought the elevators were that way. I'm reeee-ally glad you caught me." Sara sheepishly stepped onto the elevator.

"Like you said, 'excellent—"

"You look rested, by the way," she interrupted. "A good look for you."

"Oh, thanks? I just woke up from a nap." Michael stopped talking and watched Sara move her finger over the elevator's control panel. "We're on floor five."

Sara looked up with a silly grin. "Just testing you. I gotta slow my brain down."

"Like I said, I'm heading out to grab a bite," Michael stated. "Maybe that would help with your rushing mind."

"While food would be nice, a nap is needed. Especially since I plan on attending your presentation tonight. We can always head out after that."

"Sure thing."

"Can you believe it? Last one before we're off to California! So exciting!"

"Yeah." A crooked smile crawled across Michael's face. "I'm look-ing forward to tonight. Last presentation on this leg of the trip. Feels somehow special to me. Like something was accomplished."

"Look at that smile. You almost look cocky," Sara noted as the elevator stopped.

Michael shrugged. "I don't know about that. Just feeling good about tonight. Hope for one more good connection with the audience before packing up the tents."

"You'll nail it. You might be on the stage, but you're one of them. That's why they like you."

When the elevator doors opened, Michael gestured for Sara to step off first, and she stumbled into the hall. "Well, thanks for helping me find the elevator. I would have been wandering the lobby like some lost soul without you."

"I'm sure you would have made it eventually. You're a semi-capable adult, after all. Let me help you with your suitcase."

"About time," Sara teased. "I thought you were a gentleman."

"I just didn't want to give the impression that I thought you needed assistance."

"Assist away. I hate dragging that thing. Slows me down!" She bolted down the hall, pleased to be relieved of the burdensome suitcase.

"You could show your gratitude by waiting for me," Michael said as he endeavored to keep pace.

Sara snapped authoritatively. "Not happening. Chop, chop! Keep up."

"Is this what happens when you spend time with your son?"

"No." Sara stopped walking and smiled back at Michael. "In the end, I think I just like people doing what I say. It's a flaw."

"Perhaps. Enjoyed your time with your son, though?"

"Absolutely. Thanks for checking in, by the way. I appreciated it."

"No problem."

"Well, sir," Sara proclaimed with overemphasized formality, "I have made it to my room. I think. This is my room, right?" A smile and a nod from Michael let Sara know she remembered correctly. "Thank you for the escort." She jutted her right hand forth, thumb pointing directly at the ceiling.

Michael took and rotated her hand so her palm faced the floor.

He raised it and planted a light kiss. "It was a pleasant walk, madam," he replied after the gentle gesture.

A small gleam, like the reflection of starlight on the ocean, briefly sparkled in her eyes, and she slowly pulled her hand from Michael's fingers. "That's not getting you a tip," she said through a warm smile. "I will see you tonight, though."

"If not a tip, maybe you will buy the first round?"

"That could be."

"Enjoy your nap." Michael held the door open to allow Sara to pull her luggage across the threshold.

"Oh, I will," Sara assured. "Enjoy your lunch."

"No doubt," Michael eased the door shut. Dueling forces competed in his stomach. One sought to feel light, and the other longed to clench itself into a tight knot. Neither had any sway over how his heart felt as he returned to the elevator.

CHAPTER 18
MOLTING

Michael made his way to the center of the stage and looked out at his audience. It had been a good night. He and Brian, in preparation for future presentations, incorporated more music than usual in the evening. Michael's concerns that the increased musical interludes would dilute his message and personal connection were quickly assuaged as he seamlessly wove his words with the selected passages. Now he prepared to deliver his final thoughts, not just of the evening but also on this leg of his promotional tour.

"So, here we are," Michael said, "nearing the end of our time together. I must confess to feeling a little extra—moved—at the moment. Can't quite tell if I'm sad, excited, expectant, or nostalgic. I suppose I'm a mix of all that. You see, we've been in this area for over two weeks, living out of a Hyatt Hotel and driving fifty miles this way and thirty miles that way to meet with fine audiences almost every night. We'll be traversing the country in two days, flying to California."

"Lucky man!" a voice called from the audience.

A thoughtful smile rose and faded when Michael looked at the speaker. "Could be, but don't discount this moment either. I'm lucky to be here, talking about dreams and the fear, the very real fear, created by chasing them . Man, Bruce knew what he was saying. These presentations, they are part of a dream an eight-year-old Michael Tanner had. A little boy who just wanted to be an author. I guess I can look back at that kid and say, 'Thanks for dreaming,' and he can look at me and say, 'Thanks for working to make it real. For not giving in to the fear and doubt.' That's a pretty good conversation. A damn good conversation. It also conveys my belief in both the power and powerlessness of words.

"You see, that's what my talks with you are always about. Regardless if I'm focusing on this idea or that idea, one thing remains: the power of words. The power words have to inspire, to help us dream, to help us reach across the miles and simply say hello to loved ones, or to reach across a canyon of sadness to comfort someone in pain or, at the least, let them know they are not alone. Words have power. But only so much. They're not omnipotent. Words without action eventually ring hollow. They become bitter reminders of shattered dreams and halfhearted efforts. Of our failures.

"The key, therefore, is combining great effort with our words in the pursuit of goals and dreams. It has been said that the whole point of, um, the spiritual life, for want of a better term—and of spiritual words—is to bear fruit in your life. There should be some manifestation of certain words in your life. How those words guided you, comforted you, inspired you, helped you hold on when you didn't want to, and gave you the ability to express joy when that time came. And it doesn't matter if that spiritual part of you is fed by the words of Buddha or the songs of Bruce; just let it be nurtured, people!"

A spontaneous cheer rose from the crowd. Michael raised his arm and shook his head, quickly quieting his audience. Sara, seated near Brian in the back of the room, looked at her boss and smiled. "How long did it take him to write this? They are in the palm of his hand."

He hesitated before speaking, misgivings slowly growing to certainty. "Well, crap, I don't know. He takes hours to plan his presentations, but he's been off the cuff since that guy called him lucky."

"No way. Really?" Sara whispered.

Brian kept his eyes locked on the stage. "Just ripping open his chest. It usually works out for him."

"That's the essence of all my presentations," Michael pointed at Brian, "that you have to take the words that make up your dreams and act on them. Daily. That's how a life can be transformed. That's how fear is overcome. I believe that the greatest danger to the human spirit is stagnation. The desire, the yearning, to be transformed is the soul's cry when stagnation sets in. So I would like to end tonight by focusing our attention, one last time, on the anchors that weigh us down, the chains that bind, and with any luck, a few words to raise us up.

"I think sometimes there comes a point where we recognize how our decisions have impacted our lives. How some flaws, be they impatience, lack of focus, selfishness, whatever, have taken root when we weren't looking. Lao Tzu famously taught that the ignorant blame others and avoid responsibility while the wise seek answers and reconciliation. The problem in that process is one does not move easily from ignorance to wisdom. There are many miles to walk on that journey, a trek made more difficult by the shame we feel when we recognize those flaws. The great, great philosopher, Bruce Springsteen, taught this in the song 'Badlands.' He articulated that pain we have all felt. That pain deep inside, in our hearts, that we just want to get rid of. In 'One Step Up,' he lamented the disgust caused when we realize, when we really see, the fact we are not who we wished we were. We missed the correct path somewhere and just, um, slipped I think is the word he used. We slipped up.

"One thing in particular I like about the previous line is the word 'slipped.' He didn't plummet. Didn't career. Didn't crash like an out of control freight train! Just slipped. Yet, how often do our slips become freefalls? Our flaws become irreversible shortcomings? The reason is found in our minds. Our perceptions of our lives. Faulty perceptions become imprisoning realities. Both Bruce and the Buddha knew that. The Boss tells us in 'Living Proof' that an open cage can be a prison. All it takes to imprison someone are the shadows of the past, and those shadows are often stronger than steel bars. The Buddha taught that the most effective prisons are not made of iron. Rope does not create the worst knots. The strongest walls are not made of wood. It's the pleasure you take in gold and jewels. The mental attachments you make to material items and self-defeating thoughts are the most difficult bonds to break. Can you find the strength to snap those fetters?

"Before we tackle that question, let's take stock of where we are. I realize I might be painting a rather bleak picture at the moment. It is also a place many people find themselves in either because of our flaws, our fears, the shadows of our past, or the false attachments—gold and jewels—we make in a desperate search for meaning. Likely a combination of all three. Our prisons are constructed by these forces. We may be trapped, but with effort and hope we can free ourselves One thing's for sure: you can't get free if you don't acknowledge where you are. You can't overcome what you flee. You can't improve what you ignore.

"So, how do we break free? How do you shed that skin in which you no longer belong? I don't care what your struggle is, I guarantee you've shown your mettle in one area of your life, and you can bring those qualities to the darkness. Strength. Courage. Insight. Forgiveness. And the real blessing is you don't have to do it alone. Trusted friends can help you on the path. Don't be afraid to reach out.

Somewhere deep inside of you is the voice of some member of your family, your circle of friends, or your fellowship who planted a seed of strength in you. Let that seed flourish. Loved ones you want to make proud and loved ones who wish you well are with you now, even while you stand seemingly alone again in the majesty of the storm. Who knows? Maybe a book like *The Dhammapada* or that favorite song might just have the words, those magic words, to give you some faith so you can shed your skin and become that great, great person that your friends already know you are. Imagine how much better off you might be if you allow yourself to believe in the compliments of your friends. If you look at yourself through their eyes, you might find someone worthy of rising up and helping others do the same. I wish you all well. Keep fighting the good fight with all thy might!"

The audience cheered as Michael waved to them. His eyes sought Brian and Sara, who were standing and clapping. Brian stopped clapping and shrugged his shoulders, silently asking what had possessed Michael to go so far from his planned conclusion. A quick gesture communicated Michael's desire to talk later that evening. Brian was more than happy to oblige.

All that we are is the result of what we have thought: it is founded
on our thoughts, it is made up of our thoughts.
If a man speaks or acts
with a pure thought, happiness follows him, like
a shadow that never leaves him.
-The Buddha, *The Dhammapada*, chapter 1

CHAPTER 19
STEPPING FORWARD

"That could have gone better," Michael repeated. "I think I got lost in my own thoughts during the conclusion."

Brian, Sara, and he were tucked into a comfortable booth located in an isolated corner of Kells. The booth could easily accommodate six people, giving Michael ample room to sprawl across one wide side with a leg on the seat while the other was planted on the floor. Sara and Brian occupied the other: Brian seated directly across from Michael with Sara to his right. They were two drinks into their conversation, and the author was still displeased with the evening.

"The conclusion could have gone better—"

"I knew it," interrupted the sour-faced author.

"Could have," reiterated Brian emphatically. "The body of the presentation, however, went very well."

"But you agree, not the conclusion?"

"Fuck, you've got a one-track mind right now. Tell me, what am I agreeing to?" Brian asked.

"I don't think a clear message was delivered when I went off script," Michael stated.

"Not good enough," Brian responded. "Be specific. Where do you think you lost your clarity? Give me an example."

Michael silently reviewed his presentation, his face lighting up when he found his evidence. "I got it. I was trying to make a point about fears being obstacles and how past decisions or failures can trip us up. Then brought in the Buddhist idea of false attachments before trying to wrap it up with a Springsteen lyric. I claimed to give three examples but it might have been four. Hell, I was the one who said it, and I can't keep track!"

"Enough," Brian proclaimed, "You are splitting hairs here. We can write it out later and decide if it was three or four. The point is the overall lesson you presented was strong."

"Not if people can't understand the jabbering jester before them. I didn't even have a clear message."

Sara shook her head and sighed. "You really are a bit blind right now. There was a real message in what you talked about. Heartfelt and sincere, which people like. You may have surprised the audience by going a little dark in the conclusion, but no clear message? I disagree completely."

"I'm with Sara," Brian said. "Let's face it: Sara and I were audience members for most of the conclusion. We were hearing it for the first time. I did find myself wondering where you were going, but I got the point by the time you finished."

"Absolutely," Sara agreed. "Plus, you had some great lines. One in particular: 'Imagine how much better off you might be if you allowed yourself to believe in the compliments of your friends.' That was good."

"Was it?" Michael smirked and stared at Sara who returned his gaze with an arched eyebrow.

"No doubt," Brian responded. "The part about the word 'slipped' from the Springsteen song was something I liked, too. But I can see how you wish it were a little tighter. Maybe flowed a little bit better from the bulk of the presentation."

"That's it. And I can't do that in the larger presentations. The ones that will be recorded. I need to be more disciplined during those," Michael complained.

Brian nodded in agreement. "You do, especially with the choreographed optics and music. But you can't plan yourself to the loss of some of your spontaneity. That keeps you loose and keeps that connection with the audience, um, word please."

"Authentic," Sara snapped, casting a supportive gaze upon Michael. "The wall between you, the presenter, and them, the audience, is very permeable at times. You want to keep that."

"Oh yeah. I also think you should start putting together some notes on that idea you shared—about words and actions combining to, ah, transform a life. Put your own twist on that, and you have your follow-up hit," Brian mused.

Michael finished the final swig of his Guinness, "Could be."

"You good?" Brian asked. "I mean, you're still thinking about things, but generally speaking, feel good? In all honesty, you should."

Michael attempted to agree. "Yeah, I think so. I just hope the audience wasn't too disappointed."

"Forty-five minutes of Q&A after the presentation. Then that group you sat with in the lobby for another twenty. Believe me, the most disappointed person in the room was you," retorted Brian. "You did fine. I am going to get rolling. Meeting in my room at 10:00. Our last media obligations are in the afternoon and wheels up for California the next morning."

Sara shimmied out of the booth to allow Brian to depart. He dropped forty dollars on the table. "You guys can cover the rest. Have a good night."

When Sara sat back down, she looked at the still brooding author. "It went fine."

Michael hesitated. "I guess." Sara cocked her head to the side and gave him a stern glare. "Okay. It went well, but I am still surprised by where I went. Couldn't tell if I was talking to the audience or myself."

"Glad you mentioned that. I liked what you were saying but, as an audience member," Sara paused when she referred to herself that way, "I couldn't help but feel you were pulling from either personal experience or aspiration. Wasn't sure which one. I just know this: what you present is more than some intellectual exercise. That's obvious."

"Didn't realize I was so transparent. What else do you see?"

Sara sipped her drink, her brow furrowed while she swung her leg onto the seat. "Not as much as you think. It's clear you've got a lot going on up there. I have no idea what or why. You have a certain ability to obscure the view. I'm not even sure you mean to or if it's just second nature to you."

"That's interesting. Though I wonder, are you describing me, or have you started describing yourself?"

"Hey," Sara put forth her hand like she was blocking the question, "talking about you here! Leave me out of it."

"Don't run and hide," Michael teased. "You know I have a point."

"So you think."

Sara's deadpanned response caused Michael to slow down the conversation. "Okay. Let's say I concede your point about me. That does not negate the fact that description might fit you."

"I'll allow that."

"Very gracious of you. Anyway, I think the same thing applies to much of my writing. My presentations. I have not accomplished much in the most important realms of life and, when discussing aspirations, I could well be seeking to inspire myself as much as anyone. However, I don't think people of Melissa's ilk want to promote someone as a bumbling work in progress."

"Screw Melissa and her ilk," Sara shot back, pleased with the conversation's new direction. "And how are you bumbling? I mean, you write, you speak, you keep in touch with your daughters. Look around this place. You know how many men in here I would trust sitting across from me? None. If you're a 'work in progress,' the world should have more people working like you do."

Michael leaned back on his side of the booth "Well, that's very nice of you to say—"

"And there it is."

"There what is? You didn't even let me finish my sentence."

"You pulled back from my compliment. Trying to close down the conversation. You," Sara pointed her finger at Michael and tapped the air with her final three words, "obscured the view."

"Fine, meaning I may have," Michael confessed. "Of course, maybe I'm just trying to create an irresistible air of mystery about me."

"Yeah, well, maybe it's an air of annoyance. Ever think about that?"

Michael laughed, his usual amusement with Sara's wit. "That is a possibility. I also wonder about your bad breakup. Care to share?"

"No, no, no." Sara shook her head as she repositioned herself. "This is about your flaws, not mine."

"That and you haven't had enough to drink yet, right?"

"It's official—you're annoying."

"Why's that? Because I listened to you and remembered what you said from a previous conversation?"

"Well, when you put it like that, it almost sounds flattering," Sara confessed. "Let me just say it was someone I should have left quicker than I did but am VERY happy to be rid of."

"Sounds like you made a difficult and, dare I say, heroic decision."

"Heroic?"

"I imagine this person did not make the departure easy. That there was struggle involved. And here you are smiling and laughing. A caring mother and a successful professional. Heroic."

Sara looked down, and she attempted to allow Michael's claim to settle into her thoughts. It drifted along her consciousness, seeking and being denied traction. Heroic. The word would not be ignored. She raised her gaze to meet Michael's. "You may be overstating things, but thanks."

"You may have a hard time accepting compliments," Michael noted. "I do hope you don't let this man, whoever he is, obscure your view of yourself."

"Well, your presentation tonight rang true for me. But I'm working on it. Sound good?"

Michael raised his glass. "Sounds good."

Sara touched her beer bottle to Michael's mug. "Which does not mean I wish to discuss it further." Her voice made it perfectly clear the conversation was done.

"Fair enough." Michael's mind quickly found a far more relaxing topic. "We're heading to California soon. Beach or wineries?"

"Now you're talking! Why choose? Both!"

"I guess I was asking about your preference."

"Got it. Since it's autumn—winery! I love wine."

"As opposed to other forms of alcohol?"

"Point taken. Doesn't change the fact I love wine. You should write a wine book so I can help you with the research."

The two transitioned into a conversation about wine and writing with tepid forays into faulty perceptions and flaws.

CHAPTER 20
FACING A DEMON

Michael looked at the time on his cell phone. Midnight. As good a time as any to begin the process of seeking four hours of sleep. At least it had been a good night. It was rewarding to sit with Brian and Sara, to have the opportunity to see his presentation through their eyes. They calmed his professional anxiety and helped him look to the future. His professional road was much clearer than the personal path he sought. How he wished the fog would lift, but there was only one way that would happen. *Unworthy coward. Impotent oaf.* Such thoughts in the last of his waking minutes did not portend a restful sleep.

***

An oppressive darkness pushed against Michael's chest when he entered the gym. So much darker than usual. No street lights. No lightning flashes to illuminate the horror. Lord, it was dark. He stepped hesitantly over the threshold. Caution proved pointless as Michael tripped over the dumbbells he envisioned strewn across the floor.

He remained where he fell, a listless heap. What else to do? Fighting, fleeing, hiding? All seemed pointless. There was no escape. All that was available were various forms of defeats. Why bother?

Yet for reasons he never truly understood, he rose, only to step on another dumbbell and fall to the floor. Stumbling in the dark. Perfect. But then a street lamp shimmered to life, followed by another. Shafts of light invaded the gloom, casting a spotlight on dancing dust and stagnant decay. One of three lamps above the ring also flickered to life, straining to pierce the black veil. The light was enough, just enough, to allow Michael to scan the room. It was not dumbbells that caused him to fall; it was bodies. Broken and dismembered bodies. Arms ripped from shoulders lay on the floor. A head hung where a speed bag should have been. *Do I know you?* A punching bag was a human torso spared the burden of carrying its limbs. A man with a hole punched through his chest, a victim of a ruthless beating, lay prone in the ring. Lungs and a heart were in a bucket by his side.

Is this my end? Dismantled by this beast? Michael continued to search the room. The same. Always the same. No weapon to fend off the horror. No sanctuary. Just the waiting. Waiting for the inevitable. For doom. *Please don't make me wait much longer. Please finish this.*

The creature smashed through the floor some fifteen feet to his left. Michael looked at the creature and then the bodies all around him. His focus returned to the beast. He froze, his palms raised facing the heavens. Desperate eyes pleaded with his tormentor. *What do you want from me?* The answer came in a crushing blow to Michael's stomach. The beast held him up solely for the pleasure of unleashing another thunderous body blow. A fist then hammered down, driving Michael to the floor. The creature roared its fury, shaking the building if not the earth itself. Michael spit blood while he attempted to find his feet. It was a wasted effort. Two more hammering blows. Another murderous bellow. The creature lifted Michael and hurled him through the wall.

Landing in a bedroom, he recognized it even with the crushed bodies littering the space. The Door was not present here like it had been before. *Where was it? Why did it even matter? Wait, the body on the bed? Dead? Who is it? Is that a woman? I can't see her. Is it? No! Please no.*

The creature burst into the room to find Michael crawling over shattered limbs toward the bed. Hoisted like a rag doll yet again, Michael crashed through a window, coming to rest on the deserted street. Rain poured from the skies and washed the blood he lost down the road to the sewer grate, a stream of life flowing from his being to a final underground home. Michael rose to all fours. *Why am I here again?* Michael begged the rain for an answer. None was forthcoming. He raised a fist and struck the street in frustration. A splashing puddle was the reward of his might. *Again and again. Here to be tortured?* Another blow for the asphalt to ignore. *Again and again. To be humiliated?* Another ineffective strike accompanied by the fearsome arrival of the creature, leaping from the building to the ground. Michael looked at his foe, eyes pleading for answers. *Why must we do this again and again? What do you want from me?!*

"What do you want?!" Michael hollered from his knees, his plaintive question now a rage-filled demand. Tilting his head back, he screamed his fears and frustrations to the heavens. The sound was more beast than man as Michael's emotions flowed unchecked. His attention turned to his monstrous foe, which was content to stand and watch Michael's futile display of anger.

Fuck you! What do you want?! To repeatedly beat me? I'm right the fuck here! Come on! Do it again! Michael's fists renewed an assault of the pavement with feral intensity. To his surprise, the asphalt cracked under the power of his blow. And something else.

Something much deeper in his soul was shaken. Somewhere, hope rose from anger, and love combined with rage. A child's ideals and dreams overwhelmed the years of fears as the kaleidoscope of his life twisted the experiences of a lifetime into a moment. Tears that defied description formed in his eyes. Choking on a lump in his throat, Michael's gaze turned upward to witness rolling storm clouds, vanguards of dangerous days and destruction. They seemed impenetrable, perhaps at one time they were, but now beacons split the gloom. Guitars roared and horns blew. Drums pounded and ancient voices loosed battle cries. A signal lit the sky calling for heroes while lightning flashed, bringing the strength of Eitri and Brokkr's creation into Michael's body.

He did not wipe the tears that flowed but chose to simply confront his enemy. *Again! Yes, again!* His fist fell like a hammer and a crack ran the length of the street. The unrelenting beast loosed a war cry. Michael's answer came in a simple whisper. *No surrender.*

Michael charged. One blow after another caused the creature to step backwards, stunned by the power suddenly coursing through Michael's veins. It kicked Michael away, which sent him skittering across the street. Michael rose, eyes crazed. Manic. *Again!* He charged his tormentor, fingers ripping apart the stone and dirt that comprised the creature's body. For the first time in all their encounters, the beast felt pain. The earth shook and buildings splintered while the combatants exchanged ground-shaking blows, neither granting mercy nor quarter. The beast, seeking space, lifted Michael and hurled him back into the lodgings adjacent to the gym.

He was on his feet almost before he landed. He scanned the room. The bodies were gone. *Where? Who were they?* Racing to the window, he saw the beast leaping toward him. Undaunted, he elected to launch himself like a missile to intercept the creature. They plummeted to the pavement, twin meteors in a celestial dance of destruction. The beast rose, dirt and stone falling from its body, shorter than it had ever been. It bellowed. Angry. Wrathful. Confused.

Again! Michael charged. Pounding. Kicking. Ripping at the body of his foe. Bone-crushing fists fell on Michael's back. They gave him pause, but Michael was unrelenting. Fearsome and ferocious. The beast used its bulk to toss Michael away so it could unleash its vines. The weapons struck true, tearing into Michael's chest. With a growl borne from some deep pit in his soul, he ripped the tendrils out of the creature's body. The fresh sores from whence the vines were pulled oozed a brown liquid. Michael tore the projectile from his body. *Again!* The creature snorted and turned, disinterested in continuing. It lumbered toward the alley where Michael had hidden in the dumpster. Where he merged with trash. Where he became filth.

Michael ran around the corner, pulling up short when he saw the creature standing before the Door from the deep. The Door pulsed as if a terrible force was straining against it. The beast looked at Michael and snorted again. A sudden gust of wind rose behind Michael, whipped down the alley, blew through the creature, and lifted dirt and grime into a swirling dust storm. The wind swayed and bent like a thing alive, ripping more pieces off the beast. Michael watched. Uncertainty was the reward for his vision. The beast looked at him and, for the last time, sniffed as the wind pulled it apart and propelled the particles through the cracks and crevices of the Door.

No! We're not done! No! Michael raced to the Door. It looked just like it did in the deep. Every engraving. Every knot in the wood. The swooping arch and the doorknocker were all there. Everything. Michael's eyes found the doorplate. It was empty. Wait. It shimmered, a dim light dancing across a brass surface. Names flashed. Some too fast to read. Others vacillated before being replaced. Douglas. Abraham. Lee. Mary. Ken. Bruce. Names, decades old. Why? Jennifer. Fred. William. Even Kate. And more. Many more.

The procession slowed. Jay. Mary. Lucy. Brian. Barry. Carol. Sara. Her name lingered for an extra heartbeat before fading. Michael.

He stared at his name which was slowly being burned onto the nameplate. Tentatively a trembling hand reached for the handle. *Should I pull it open? Is it time?* He grabbed the ring and found his fingers burned by an unearthly cold. Grunting in pain he fell to one knee. He rose to try again only to be turned away by searing heat.

***

Michael woke up, both of his arms reaching above his chest like he was bench pressing air. He gasped for breath. *Okay. Okay. What the fuck? Okay. I was at the Door. Ready to open it. Why couldn't I?* He stood up and paced the room. *Because I was asleep. I need to do it now. Awake. Fully aware of what I'm doing.* Drawing a deep breath and then another, Michael sat on the floor. The time had come. The Door had to be opened, come what may.

"Therefore, Junah, rest in me. Enter the Field
Like a warrior. Purged of ego, firm in Discipline,
seeking no reward save the stroke itself.
Give the shot to me....Now strike my friend, as I have taught you.
Hold nothing back."
-Steven Pressfield, *The Legend of Bagger Vance*

But the ignorant, faithless, doubting self goeth
to destruction...who hath cloven asunder doubt by wisdom,
who is ruled by the Self, actions do not bind him...
Therefore, with the sword of the wisdom of the Self cleaving asunder
this ignorance-born doubt dwelling in thy heart,...
Stand up, O Bharata.
-The Bhagavad Gita, chapter 4:40-42

CHAPTER 21
OPENING THE DOOR

"Anyone want to help me get some books from the storage room?"

Hands were raised all around Sister Patty's third grade Sunday school classroom. Not, despite what Sister Patty claimed, because the students were all "angelic." Some delusions help people get through the day; some projections may even take root. But no, the chance to leave the room, to get a walk, to do most anything but stay in that room was the primary motivator. There were plenty of hands for Mr. Smith to choose from. His eyes found young Michael Tanner, who had neither a hand nor his eyes raised. "How about you, young man?" Mr. Smith's invitation was sent with a wide smile shining from the middle of his bearded face. "Can you help me out?"

Sister Patty clapped her hands gently together, blessing Mr. Smith's instincts. "Oh, an excellent choice. Michael is a fine boy. Go help Mr. Smith, Michael."

Sheepishly, the shy boy rose from his chair and accompanied Mr. Smith.

***

This was the first memory Michael encountered as he prepared to open the Door. The walk itself was beyond his conscious grasp. He knew they crossed the street, walking from St. Christopher's Catholic School to The Cathedral of St. Christopher, but what was said or felt when they approached the door to the cathedral's basement was also forgotten. The stairs, however: those stairs were planted in his mind like a memorial on a field of battle. Well, not exactly. It wasn't the stairs. It was Mr. Smith's pants that could still be seen. So neatly pressed. So clean. Slowly descending with Michael into the basement. The books, Michael was assured, were in an alcove in the far corner of the expansive room. It was there that Mr. Smith steered Michael to pick up the non-existent books.

It was because of that alcove, because of what happened there, that Mr. Smith's hands were recalled with vivid details. There was a little bit of hair on his knuckles but the hands had no scars. The fingers weren't terribly long, but they were thick. Mr. Smith wore two rings, a wedding band and a ring on his other hand. Then the hands moved, caressing Michael. Sculpting him.

Michael stood still, paralyzed. Wasn't Mr. Smith a nice man? People liked him. What was happening? Then the voice. Whispering. Encouraging. Michael was told he was a good boy and that his body was healthy. A gift from God. It's supposed to work that way. When it gets hard, it just means you're strong. Was Michael hugged? Held from behind. Something rubbed against Michael's back.

What is happening? Maybe it'll stop soon. Mr. Smith isn't talking anymore. Just breathing. Breathing. Something's rubbing against me. I don't...I don't...understand any of this. I don't...I don't...I don't.... Then he thanks me. Tells me I'm a good boy and that this will be our secret. Good boys keep secrets, don't they? Okay. Yes. I can keep a secret. I promise. I just want to leave this basement. I can keep a secret. Just let me leave.

Michael returned to Sister Patty's room and finished class. Next, the walk home.

What to tell mommy? Nothing. I can't. I made a promise. Besides I'm mommy's rock. That's what she calls me, ever since dad left. I help her stay strong. I help her with my brother and sister. I can't tell her because she needs me to be her rock. And I'm a good boy. I help her with my younger brother and sister. Good boys keep their promises.

Thus, a decision was made to honor a promise. A promise made to a man utterly undeserving of loyalty. Of fidelity. Of good faith. A promise kept for a quarter century.

The events in that basement were never mentioned, buried in the bedrock of Michael's soul. How the desire to protect the memory and, as time passed, to allow it to be forgotten impacted his life would never be completely known. That it impacted his life was irrefutable.

How does a life go on when all a child has is confusion and shame? He only knew he couldn't tell. He had to be a rock. So he wearily went to school on Monday morning. It was less than twenty-four hours since innocence died, and life in Mrs. Boniface's third grade class had to continue. He arrived disheveled and disinterested in learning. He took his seat hoping not to be noticed.

Mrs. Boniface, however, seemed to always see everything. She strolled by Michael's desk and leaned over to whisper a conversation with her student. Truth be told, she did not lean far because she barely crossed five feet tall but to Michael, she was a giant, powerful and majestic. "Michael, are you okay? You look really tired."

"I'm good," was all Michael could mumble.

Mrs. Boniface stood unconvinced and sought for some way to push past young but powerful defenses. "Well, I think you might need a walk. Besides, your hair is a little messy. Maybe go to the bathroom and just wash up?"

Michael slinked from the room, happy to be free of Mrs. Boniface's attention, even though he always liked her. Michael thought she was the perfect blend of nice and tough. She made the students get things done and cheered them on when they plodded about. She was a good person and his favorite teacher. He just didn't want to be seen. Standing in the bathroom, he looked in the mirror. His hair was a bit messy. He put some water in his hands and ran them through his hair, pulling the mop on his head this way and patting it there until it became a much more controlled mess. Satisfied that Mrs. Boniface would be pleased, he returned to the room.

"Michael," Mrs. Boniface exclaimed, "you look wonderful. Did you have a comb with you?"

He found his seat and muttered, "No. I just used my hands and water."

"Well, you are clearly very skilled. You did a fantastic job."

"Yeah! You did do a great job!" a little girl called out from behind Michael, following her teacher's compassionate cue.

"Thanks." Michael shyly smiled, and he struggled with the idea that it was nice to be noticed.

Mrs. Boniface took her position in front of the class, chalk in hand, with bright posters hanging on the wall above her chalkboard. "Okay, okay, it is time to begin our spelling lesson."

To Michael's pleasure, the school day progressed like most others. There was a comfort in the routine, with one exception. He did not want to go to lunch with the class or go outside for recess. He couldn't think up any good excuse so, as the class lined up for lunch and prepared to be escorted by Mrs. Richardson across the hall, he approached Mrs. Boniface with his honest request. "Mrs. Boniface?"

"Yes, Michael? What can I do for you?"

Michael paused before speaking. "I just want to eat lunch by myself. Could I eat in here? And maybe, skip recess too?"

Examining Michael's face, Mrs. Boniface knew the boy didn't want to talk and definitely didn't want to be around people. She nodded and gently patted his shoulder. "Of course you can. Tell you what, I need to get my lunch and you need to get yours. Let's say we meet back here in five minutes. Okay?"

"Okay," Michael sighed, a wave of relief almost overwhelming him. *Be a rock.*

"Do you have something you want to talk about?"

"No, just like it in here."

"That's very nice to hear, Michael. Thank you."

He wasn't sure what he was being thanked for but said, "You're welcome," quickly snatched up his lunch box, and plopped himself down at the reading table in the corner of the room. Mrs. Boniface sat at her desk, and he watched her lay her lunch out as if she were on a picnic. She made it seem like lunch was special.

Pleased with her preparations, Mrs. Boniface addressed her student from across the room. "Michael. Since you don't feel like talking, I am going to play my music. You can feel free to read a book if you like. Or draw. Just use your time well."

Michael nodded, and soft jazz music filled the room. It was thirty-five minutes before either of them spoke. "Mrs. Boniface?" Michael looked up from the picture he drew of a Martian eating a spaceship.

"Yes, Michael?"

"Can I go outside for recess?"

"Sure. There's about ten minutes left. You won't get much playing in."

"That's okay. This was fun."

"Yes, it was." Mrs. Boniface's face shone as she spoke. Michael thought she looked like a bright moon on a gentle summer night.

Michael went outside and walked the large loop around the play area. He did not interact with classmates or even attempt to join the games. He just strolled and allowed the early fall sun to warm his face. When the students were called in by the teachers on recess duty, he meandered to the end of the line and progressed with his class back to Mrs. Boniface's room for the afternoon activities, which included that day's special—music.

The class returned from music and held their end of the day meeting before preparing for dismissal. Michael packed quickly and scurried to his teacher's side. "Mrs. Boniface. I really liked that music you played at lunch. It's way better than our music class."

"Well, it's important to hear all kinds of music, Michael, so don't be too hard on poor Ms. Cummings."

Michael was nervous that he had upset his teacher. "Oh, I wasn't trying to be mean. I—"

"I know," Mrs. Boniface empathetically interjected. "It's fine. If you liked the music that much, why don't you take my album home with you? I have plenty more."

"You would let me? That's so cool!"

"Just be careful with it." Mrs. Boniface handed the LP to Michael. She smiled as she saw Michael, for the first time that day, look truly happy.

He marveled at the mix of colors on the cover and the musicians with their exotic instruments. Never had he seen the likes of them before. Looking up at her, he exclaimed for the second time, "So cool! Thanks!"

"You're welcome, Michael. Perhaps we will do lunch again."

The bus ride after school was eternal, and he wanted nothing more than to get home and play the LP in his room. When he got off the bus and walked the short path to his home, the excitement of the album collided with the revolting memory of yesterday's walk. Yet again, he had to fight off tears to protect his mother from his horror.

He entered the house to a soft but loving greeting from his mother. "Michael, how was—what's that you have?"

"Mrs. Boniface gave me this record to listen to. It's really neat. I—"

His mother interrupted. "That's nice, Michael. Both your siblings are sleeping. It's a miracle. So if you want to listen to the album in your room, just keep the volume a little low, okay?"

"Sure, Mom." Michael started to head to his room before he turned to offer an invitation. "You wanna listen with me?"

"No, thank you. Someone's got to keep this house clean. Maybe you can help me later."

"I will. I promise," Michael said quickly. "Okay if I go to my room?"

"Yup. Have fun, dear."

Michael sat in his room and quickly got the jazz album spinning. The horns moved him in ways he couldn't explain. The drumming, sometimes gentle and other times promising excitement, caused his head to bob and feet to tap. The plucking of bass strings touched the golden cord that runs through the human soul to heaven and back to connect to others. There was something magical in the rhythms he heard. A saxophone's lonely tale brought another round of tears to his eyes even as he learned, alone in his room and lost in a bevy of confusing thoughts, that music has the power to speak to pain, which is why it also has the power to heal.

***

A group of teenagers were gathered outside the locked door at the back of St. Christopher's Catholic School. Another Sunday, another day of confirmation classes.

"Why am I here?" one young man asked his friend. "I mean, do you wanna be here?"

"Nah, but my folks want me here, so, y'know." A shrug of the shoulders accompanied the unenthused response.

"Well," the first speaker answered, "at least Mr. Smith is here. I like that guy."

"Yeah, he's pretty cool. He always lets us out early. He's a teacher but he gets it."

"He's an asshole," groused a sixteen-year-old Michael Tanner.

"What?" the first speaker asked. "You best take that back, Tanny."

"Fuckin' right," the second boy said, following the lead of his alpha. "Mr. Smith is fuckin' awesome."

Other boys, also fans of Mr. Smith and of the group's social hierarchy, closed around Michael. He hardly noticed because his attention was completely on their leader. "Sorry I offended you. Let me rephrase. Mr. Smith is a fuckin' asshole, and you're a dickhead who's too fuckin' stupid to see it."

"Oh, Tanny," the alpha crowed, anger coursing through his veins.

"If I didn't think you would just run away, I would be kicking your ass right now."

One of the oddest features of St. Christopher's was a wooden platform attached to the back of the building. It was about six inches off the ground, creating an eight-by-eight raised square. The small square was surrounded by two parallel metal rails. A rusted gate was held shut by a corroded padlock. Whatever it was for was a mystery to the boys. What it had become was well-known. If you wanted to fight, really fight someone, you stood in the square and challenged your foe to join you. Classic beatings from that square were the stuff of St. Christopher's legend. The name 'Tanny' wasn't even out of the alpha's mouth when Michael turned to enter the square, changing the mood of the moment.

"Shut the fuck up and step in," Michael challenged from the center of the ring. The tempest under his calm demeanor froze the crowd. When his opponent hesitated, Michael dug in. "Nervous? Bring your fuckin' friend in with you. Bring two. I could give a shit."

All eyes locked on Michael before glancing at his suddenly tentative foe. A car pulled up. Out bounded Mr. Smith. "Sorry I'm late, everybody. Got held up in traffic."

The crowd quickly dissipated.

"You're lucky Mr. Smith showed up," hissed the alpha, his courage renewed by the fact he didn't have to do anything. Mr. Smith unlocked the door and turned to Michael, still standing in the schoolyard ring. "Everything okay, Michael?" Mr. Smith asked.

Michael's soul snarled.

***

Time, the irresistible juggernaut, maintained its eternal march. Years passed. Fear, anger, and shame were all held in a compartment deep within Michael's being. They would arise, often when people grew too close. When someone mattered too much. Longing for and terrified of connection for fear that love would demand too much. A close circle of friends and an even tighter ring of confidants was all he needed. But people crave other things. Sometimes broken people wish to be whole, even when their scars are ignored until the point of oblivion. Laughter. Joy. Connection. Companionship. These are yearned for even by those quite adept at walking with pain. So it was that Michael married. Had children. Built a career and built a life.

Marriages can deepen. A spouse can burrow into one's life, even into one's hidden, inner world. As the years passed, Michael unexpectedly developed increasing anxiety. Panic attacks. An aversion to crowds and touch. Even the touch of a beloved. A near breakdown. Rocks can shatter. Michael's body raged to remind him to heal what his mind strove to conceal.

Kate, his wife, was dismayed by what she saw. What she lived. Was this the man she married? How had she failed him? Her pain became his as his alienation became hers. An awful cycle of suffering threatened to consume them. Why couldn't he stop failing her? They could fix this, but how?

The nightmares began. The unconscious visits of his earthen tormentor. Images, long dormant, returned to the fore. Fear, anger, and shame, long imprisoned, needed to be addressed. All else had failed. Perhaps honesty with himself and with Kate could heal what other methods could not. The truth, after all, can set us free. For the first time in twenty-five years, Michael shared what happened when the Door closed, and Mr. Smith brought him to the darkness. Brought him into the basement.

The confession came in a child's voice. Michael sobbed when he recounted Mr. Smith to his wife. As pieces of the puzzle fell into place, Kate danced from compassion to guilt and back again. Hope was carried in their shared tears, but hope is fragile, and a healing journey can feel too slow. Kate had lived enough. Witnessed too much. "Why can't you just go away and get cured?" she once asked in a fit of frustration. The worse betrayals need not be physical. In that moment, Michael's failure was complete. He was utterly alone. He also knew he had been right all along. He was right not to tell his mother. He should not have told his wife. Some pain must be carried alone. The Door was strengthened.

When Kate asked him for a trial separation, Michael agreed. Whatever she hoped for in the separation did not occur. "*Why can't you go away and get cured?*" The question stabbed Michael but made him realize he needed to go away and never come back. He shocked Kate when he told her they were getting a divorce.

The painful road became an unexpected pleasure. Michael deepened old friendships and established new bonds to cherish. In conversations with Carol and Barry, he revealed his deepest shame. They unconditionally stood by his side, as did others. Their support was a most valued gift, evidence that fragile hope could withstand storms. That even rocks could course with life. He grew stronger, but the Door remained untouched. A source of dread. It was to be feared and avoided. Something to be kept in its proper place. His life need not take him there.

***

Then came Sara. More specifically, then came the book launch. They had already known each other for a number of months. Michael always admired her seemingly boundless energy and blunt honesty. It was at the book launch that things changed in one of those moments that reverberates in life.

Michael stood off to the side in an expansive ballroom while people milled about. It was a book launch, but he thought it looked like a wedding reception, the only comparison he could make. Drinks were poured and people laughed. Michael had pulled away from the crowd in order to grant himself the opportunity to take it all in. All this in the hopes of pushing a book into the public's consciousness. It was amazing.

Brian was off shaking who knows whose hand, but it was likely someone important. Planting new seeds for future ventures or confirming the well-laid road.

Michael had never been part of such an event. His previous two books, one fiction and one nonfiction, were picked up by small publishers and hit the publishing world with the force of a single rain drop. Idea Publishing, however, put their weight and prestige behind Michael's third book. Such efforts included an organized, strategic book launch, four to five weeks of grassroots promotions, and several national media spots, all leading into an envisioned successful national promotional tour.

"How you holding up?" Sara's voice snapped Michael from his trance. He looked into her shining eyes and smiled.

"This is amazing," Michael replied, an unintended awe gripping his voice. To his surprise, he took her hand and spun her around, pushing her away and then pulling her back in. "And I feel great." Michael danced a half-turn with Sara and twirled her out again. When he prepared to bring her back, she looked at him and laughed. And it happened. The room melted away. There was no one else present. Just him and those eyes, beautiful and mysterious like the sea. A smile more intoxicating than any drink served and a laugh that spread as music. Michael drew her back, and the two danced another half-turn before Sara, still smiling, stepped away and laughed again.

"Easy," she reprimanded playfully, her laughter fading out, "you're going to break my ankle in these shoes."

"Wouldn't want that. Besides, you're probably lucky I didn't step on your toes. I am not a graceful creature."

"You did okay. Kinda caught me by surprise."

"What? That's not what you came over here for?"

Sara let out a quick giggle that seemed to dance out of her heart. "No, that was not my plan."

"I'm supposed to be mingling, right?"

"Yes, you are," Sara imparted, her voice switching to her professional tone. She started to walk away from Michael, coaxing him to follow. "As am I. But thanks for the twirl."

"No problem. Thanks for not breaking your ankle." *And for stopping time.* Michael veered toward Brian, who wanted to introduce him to a group of people.

No problem. That was what Michael said. But it proved to be a problem. What happened in that wonderful second? How could that be? He spent the next three weeks trying to talk himself out of the notion that he felt anything. It was the excitement of the launch. The three drinks he had consumed. Sara's cheerful response was borne of surprise. Nothing else. Defensive walls rose, crumbled, and rose again. The idea that he, at forty-five, could be struck by such a lightning bolt was preposterous. It could not be.

Then the tour began. The increased time together. Michael's

defensive walls fell, and his affection rose. The substance of Sara, including her flaws, became a source of inner happiness for him. So much so that the nightmares returned. The forces behind the Door pounded and strained, seeking a reckoning.

***

Michael drew a deep breath and another. The swarm of memories surrounding this trip to the Door were embraced, bringing his emotions to a frightening keel. A second and third breath settled him. It was time to empty his mind, to actively recall nothing, and to meditate on the image of the Door. He would rise and fall as he would in the tumult that would surely unfold when the Door was pulled open.

With his eyes closed, he breathed deeper yet. He fell, again, into the abyss. Rock and stone ripped his body. The fear rose, and yet he endured. The safety of his shore was left behind, and the uncertainty of an open, storming sea was now his. Groping and cursing, he battled until he reached his destination. He arrived at the Door.

I stand before you, strength mixed with cowardice. Here because this is where my deepest pain lies, and I can only be as good a man as this pit allows. What will your opening do to me? I must know. I must. Some doors have to be opened, even if the road they lead to is frightful and fraught with uncertainty. You call me, after all this time, to find you here in the darkness. Daring me to enter. Wanting me to? Good lord, do you wish me whole? I do not know.

I run my hands along your rough wooden engravings. I feel images that awaken the spirit within. Heroes and gods. Images of friendship and pain. I think I understand. The wisdom of the ages engraved in wood. I feel your arch and my fingers, bloody and gnarled, find a doorplate with my name. My name. You belong to me? I carved and forged you? What a terrible labor.

Lastly, my hands come upon your door handle. It is to be pulled, for none will grant me entrance but my own courage. Would that I were Arthur before Excalibur or Thor with his magic gloves ready to hoist Mjolnir and strike down my foes. I am not such a man. But I am before you again, and I must know what I can take. All I have is the strength earned through struggle and enhanced by friends and family. Reaching for your brass ring, I tremble. It does not burn this time with either heat or cold. I am here because I needed to come back.

I brace myself as I pull.

CHAPTER 22
LOST IN THE FLOOD

The Door is driven open by the explosive forces it contains. A torrent of shame, fear, pain, failure, and doubt race over me, raging waters released by the sundering of a dam. Quickly, I find myself underwater, helpless. It is more than waters rushing free of containment. There is an undertow. This is the ocean. My ocean. Stormy and wrathful. I raise my head above the surface, gasping only to be pulled under again. The currents are too strong. Too much power for a weak man to overcome. Why did I leave my safe shore for these terrible storms? What arrogance possessed me?

I am no hero. No wanderer on a mythic quest. Yet I stay here, floundering. Fight, dammit! Find some strength. Here I am now, lost in the flood. Lost at sea. Is there another shore where I can find refuge? Are there no boats, no other travelers navigating these waters, who may find me in this, my hour of great need? Am I alone?

No. Not alone. I can swim. I can fight the current. I am not some piece of kelp to be tossed by the currents. I can fight. Struggle. Swim. For Mary and Lucy, that I may be the man they think their father is. In the end, does anything else truly matter? The thought of my children bolsters my spirits. I am not alone. Come what may, it is always they who bolster me, who keep me moving. Come what may. They are always with me as I hope I am with them. Energy courses where once it fled. For Jay, my oldest friend, who always saw strength where I saw none. A good man. A man of quiet inspiration and endless support. For Carol and Barry, that I may someday have the courage to see myself through their eyes. Why is it so hard to believe the vision of friends? Now is the time to start. To believe them. I can fight. I am not alone. I have a loyal Samwise. Companions in the trenches.

My progress is weak but I remain afloat. These forces are strong. I have fed them for years. Has this all been so I can merely get to know my enemy? To fall in the hopes of a future victory? No. Keep fighting. This is my time. The only time. The unfinished links of my destiny must be forged here. Still, I drown. I cannot continue. Should stop. I drown. I drown. I drown in eyes that don't see me. Sara? Are you here too? My mind is overthrown, and my heart has no home. The storm is getting weaker. Sara, is that you? How? What is that? A shore. A distant shore. I can make it. For Mary and Lucy. I know I can. These waters: I can navigate them. Move with them. They need not be the master of me. So tired. Just a few more strokes and I can stand. Touch the bottom and stand. Have I at least earned the right to stand in these waters?

***

Michael's eyes shot open when he ended his meditation. Gasping for breath, he fell to all fours as something deep in his stomach contracted, causing him to pant and claw with trembling arms at the carpet. He looked up, alone but not alone in his hotel room. Convulsions shook him to his core. Not knowing what to do, Michael shifted his focus back to the floor. He stared and allowed his entire reality to become nothing more than the carpet before his eyes and the sensations of his body. A knot in his stomach snapped, causing his body to loosen. Once tense arms were now gelatin, incapable of lending support. He fell to his side in a prone position, seemingly helpless on the floor. The breaking of the chains in his stomach spread upward through his shoulders until his throat was released from whatever invisible force had gripped it so forcefully. In that moment, Michael Tanner wept.

What ancient pain and undeserved shame poured out of him in those baptismal tears was unknown. He didn't try to outthink them or prevent their fall. His face contorted into a mask of confusion and pain. Some healing is ugly. Michael trembled again. He sat up and, just when he thought he was done, a fresh stream flowed from him. While he sobbed, he rose, standing now in his own waters. He walked to a chair and sat. Wiping his eyes, he slowed his mind. His breathing. He mentally checked those parts of his body that, a mere five minutes earlier, were excruciatingly tense.

Relaxed. Calmed. The Door was opened, and he endured. For the first time since he was eight, he felt stronger than the things in the deep. It had taken thirty-seven years to reach this moment. Crawling. Hiding. Laughing. Sharing. So much effort to gain a victory few would understand. Untrusting of the calm, he again searched his body with his mind, seeking tight and anxious areas. There were none.

He thought of the Door. The flood. It was still in him. Its fury not spent. But a more skillful swimmer now stood before it. One is not cured of such things. Such things are incorporated into a life. Into a life, but they need not be the guiding force of a life. A life he was free to share and face as he felt fit. Michael's life, he knew, would continue to have struggles and strife. All lives do. This life, however, would be more his than ever before.

Sara. He staggered to his bed and flopped onto it. Sara. How his affection for her had been a surprising source of inspiration. What do you tell someone who has altered your life? Helped save it? Is that too much to say? His mind raced. Grabbing his phone, he pulled up her name. He longed to contact her but to say what? What could be texted to make sense of this? What words would allow him to appear sane? The cell was returned to the nightstand. Slammed down as if a cursed totem. Still in jeans and a T-shirt, Michael pulled the covers to his shoulders. Time enough for everything later. Not now. Definitely not now.

Sleep came over Michael quickly. It was a good sleep. Deep and undisturbed. No demons came calling. No anxiety-driven 3:00 wake-up. It was not clear if peace or exhaustion enabled such deep slumber. Perhaps, on this night, it did not matter.

*...even the helpless victim of a hopeless situation, facing
a fate he cannot change, may rise above himself, may grow
beyond himself, and by so doing change himself. He may
turn a personal tragedy into a triumph.*
-Viktor Frankl, *Man's Search for Meaning*

CHAPTER 23
FIRST STEPS

What am I doing? Michael exited the park and approached St. Jude Church. He carried two black coffees in a cardboard cup holder. He was four steps across the street before he paused to survey the area. There was no rectory next to the church that could be seen. *Where?* He looked back to the side of the street he had just departed and saw a one-story stone building with a sharply manicured lawn. No fallen autumn leaves adorned the property despite the presence of multiple trees that had clearly lost a majority of their foliage. *That's where I should—*

"Wake up, idiot!"

The voice was accompanied by a blaring horn, and a car sped past. Michael looked at his feet and then the sidewalk, laughing at himself as he returned to safer ground. Thus had his entire day unfolded. While he slept through the night following his meditation, he awoke in an uncertain haze. His limbs had felt like rubber all day. His thoughts constantly reached back to the previous night. The nightmare. The meditation. The hope and the tears. What it all meant going forward. He had no recollection of the morning meeting where he both sought to speak with and avoid Sara. The floodgates of his mind may have poured out the previous night, but this private event need not be accompanied by a deluge of shared words. Fear of what may be revealed led to a zombielike trance that was not lost on either Brian or Sara.

The trembling legs on which he walked became less stable when he returned to his room following the meeting. He wept again without even being sure why. He needed to wrap his mind around last night's events while maintaining himself for the day's activity. A rare nap helped prepare him for an afternoon interview, and now his time was his. That he spent some of that time standing bewildered in the street seemed appropriate. He just knew he needed to talk to someone and in a daze, he purchased two coffees and proceeded to St. Jude. To visit Father Sylvan.

What am I doing?

Moving like he was fulfilling some prewritten script, Michael strode the concrete path to the front door of the rectory. There was but one step to ascend. So simple yet it caused Michael to pause. He shook his head, conquered Mount Molehill, and rang the bell. Some shuffling emanated from inside the abode, and a kind voice called for patience.

"Oh. Be right there. Sorry, I was just—why hello, Michael! How nice it is to see you." Father Sylvan smiled, patted the author's shoulder, and drew him across the entry. "What brings you here?"

"I, you see, I'm leaving tomorrow and just wanted to have that coffee with you. I hope you don't mind me showing up out of the blue like this."

"There you go again," Father Sylvan chided, escorting Michael into a sitting room. "Apologizing when there is no need."

Michael mounted a rather feeble defense. "I don't think I actually apologized."

Father Sylvan pointed at a chair for his guest to occupy. "Well, at the least you were fretting for no reason. I mean, this may come as a shock, but the social calendars of Catholic priests in the twenty-first century are shockingly open. Especially on Thursday nights."

"Well then, I am fortunate." Michael found himself starting to loosen up for the first time since he arrived. "Oh. I did bring coffee, though I wonder if you drink caffeine this late in the day."

"How is it?"

"Black. I assumed you would have sugar and cream to add to your liking."

"Well done! Stay here. I will grab a couple items from the pantry and get this coffee the way I like it."

Michael sat in silence in the living room. *Say something. Say what? Small talk? Why am I here?* He heard glasses clink and drawers open and shut as Father Sylvan bulled his way through cupboards.

"Alright!" Father Sylvan exclaimed when he returned to Michael. He held a tray with two glass mugs, two spoons, a small pile of napkins, a bottle of whiskey, a bottle of Bailey's Irish Cream, whipped cream, and a container of nutmeg. "This is how I drink coffee late in the day!"

"You're a good man, Father," Michael said. The two busied themselves preparing their Irish coffees, working happily but silently.

"I may well be," Father Sylvan replied once his coffee was properly prepared. "I am, however, definitely thankful to be Catholic right now."

"Why's that?"

"Oh, maybe you know this story. Given your writing, I think you will. Legend has it there was once a czar of Russia who was trying to decide what religion to promote to his people in an attempt to build cultural unity. He evaluated Buddhism, Christianity, and Islam."

A knowing smile spread across Michael's face. "Yes. The czar was leaning toward Buddhism until he learned of the Buddha's precept against drinking intoxicants. The czar could not fathom the Russian people giving up their vodka, so Russia became Christian!"

"To wine-drinking religions," Father Sylvan declared, raising his mug.

"To wine in general," Michael proposed.

"Well said, sir." Father Sylvan happily reclined in his chair.

"Do you think he was right?"

"Who?" The czar?"

"No, no. The Buddha," Michael clarified. "His precept that one should avoid intoxicants because they interfere with mindfulness and the focus needed for meditation."

"Well, I would say one should not get drunk and try to meditate. I would assume that would go poorly," Father Sylvan joked. Michael didn't respond and instead looked at his feet. Father Sylvan watched him closely, allowing Michael room to stew. "Are you okay?"

"I don't know. It's been a strange few weeks."

"I doubt that."

"I'm pretty confident it's been a strange few weeks," Michael responded, a slight annoyance in his voice.

"I don't doubt that," Father Sylvan noted. "I just can't imagine a few strange weeks just arose out of the blue without a few strange months leading up to it."

"Maybe years."

Michael's wavering voice struck Father Sylvan's ears like a dirge. "I see. I—"

"I don't know why I came here, Father. I am at a loss." Michael leaned back in his chair and scanned the room, desperately seeking clarity in the growing haze that permeated his mind. "I can't make sense of things at the moment." He communicated nothing save his confusion. His hesitancy.

Father Sylvan's compassionate eyes soaked in all the information they could. "May I finish answering your question?"

"Huh? What question?"

"About the Buddha. Intoxicants."

"Oh. I don't even know why I asked that. I just don't know what to say, so I blurted that out. It's not important. At all."

"Fair enough. But since you are at a loss, I could answer it, and we can see where that leads us."

"Sure. Go ahead, Father."

"Why, thank you. Clearly, drinking while attempting to meditate and proceed with vigor on the inner journey would be incompatible. In that regard, I see the man's point. Now, far more importantly, I think it is always important to remember the uniqueness of the individual while recognizing we are all human and do share some very important commonalities. We—people—tend to shrink away from the greatness of others even as our society increasingly promulgates the wonder of everyone."

"True," Michael concurred, "but it often seems to me to be a wonder grounded in nothing substantive."

"That could be. The Buddha, however, achieved a different level of psychological, spiritual, and emotional development than almost anyone who lived. This is unique. It is special. That, I dare say, is why his thoughts have endured over two thousand years and acts as inspiration to people unto this day."

Michael stared at Father Sylvan, who seemed to be growing in stature while he sat on his sofa. "Are you sure you're Catholic, Father? You are praising Buddha quite heavily."

"I attend, and greatly enjoy, interfaith retreats. Besides, one need not be a Celtics fan to recognize the greatness of Bill Russell. Now, and you know this, Buddha himself claimed to live a very encultured life until he was twenty-seven."

"True. He was drawn to the spiritual journey after years of living a typical life. The life of a prince, granted, but typical to that life." Michael was finding comfort in this unexpected and distracting exchange.

"Granted," Father Sylvan repeated with a wave of his hand, "through that intense dedication, an unbending will, ceaseless effort, nigh unto insatiable curiosity about the spiritual quest, and an unflinching commitment to honesty, the prince became the Buddha. Experiencing a joy and peace not found in his life as a prince. A joy he contended is the birthright of all people. A peace he contended all can experience. Intoxicants didn't help him get there, and so I can see why he says to avoid them. But his level of humanity is much more splendid than most, making it is easier to scoff than to strive. Yet we live at a time when our accepted level of dedication and kindness is inadequate to solve the basic problems of humanity."

"And we tear at our exemplars," Michael added, "in the name of showing our strength when, in fact, we are cowards. Cowards afraid to strive like they did."

Father Sylvan recoiled at the intensity with which Michael spoke the word 'cowards.' For a moment, he contemplated addressing it before tucking the urge away in favor of another thought. "But if we just let those exemplars be human, we may see more of ourselves in them and more of them in ourselves than our parochial level thinking often allow. I believe that is one of the biggest problems of my tradition."

"Well, that statement sparked my curiosity," Michael stated. "How do you mean?"

"I doubt it takes much to engage your intellectual or spiritual curiosity, Michael," Father Sylvan stated confidently. Michael seemed no more certain than earlier, but there was no doubt that his body radiated with energy granted him by the power of ideas. "Jesus is often portrayed and thought of as so transcendent, so distant, that we forget his humanity. His imminence. Consider his reaction to his baptism."

"I am not following you, Father."

"Really? We'll see about that." Father Sylvan countered before continuing his assessment. "Jesus was baptized by John the Baptist."

Michael picked up the story. "Yes. The voice of God proclaims him his son. A dove descends from Heaven."

"Poetic touches communicating a deeply powerful and subjective inner experience. Jesus' life led to a moment he did not understand. He was discombobulated by, let's say, his ascension of Solsbury Hill."

"Well played, Father."

"I know my audience," Father Sylvan responded. "Anyway, the Gospel of Mark states the spirit of God drove him to the desert for forty days and forty nights. Drove him! I love that idea. That one can be driven by the spirit of God."

"Have you experienced that?"

"I don't think so. But that's not important. What is important is this: I am quite comfortable with the idea that people can have profoundly powerful experiences that are theirs alone, and I do not have to completely understand or experience these events in order to respect them. I just try to avoid taking the experience of another and placing it into some mental box of my own creation to make me comfortable."

"'There are more things in heaven and earth, Horatio, Than are dreamt of in your philosophy.'"

"Indeed, William."

"I prefer my fans call me Mr. Shakespeare, thank you," Michael teased.

Chuckling, Father Sylvan raised his mug. "No offense meant, gentle bard. I don't doubt the Buddha experienced something I don't understand. I also don't doubt Jesus experienced something that demanded solitude of him. Demanded it of him in a way that I intellectually can comprehend but don't personally understand. Something that drove him from others, even without his consent. Some trails we walk alone."

Michael bit his lip for a second or two and then sighed. "Driven without his consent."

"Yes. We don't always understand why we go certain places or reach out to certain people. Sometimes we just need to surrender to our present circumstances and see what's what."

"Yeah," Michael whispered. He sat in silence, elbows on his knees, as he leaned forward in his seat. The silence was uninterrupted by Father Sylvan, who sipped contentedly on his Irish coffee. "Father?" Michael began, body position unchanged save for his eyes which now stared into Father Sylvan's.

"Yes, Michael."

"Does your church have a meeting hall? Some place where you maybe hold bake sales or pasta dinners or whatever?"

Father Sylvan placed his coffee on a coaster. "Yes, it's not a separate building or anything. It's in the basement of the church."

"Can we go there? I...I would like to see it. I just...I don't...."

"Of course," the Father said warmly. "No need to explain anything. I will go get the key to the stairs and take you across the street."

Michael stood while Father Sylvan exited the room. *Can't you speak?* While waiting, he circled his chair to stand in front of a window facing the street. Facing St. Jude. It was dusk but not yet dark, a slight breeze moving the branches on the tree that stood watch in the center of the front lawn. He placed his hand on the window. What he felt was a mystery to himself and to Father Sylvan, who quietly reentered the room. Michael twitched sharply despite his host's attempt to gently address him.

"Ready?"

"Yes," Michael said. "Let's go."

The two men left the rectory and walked silently to the street. Michael was not inclined to speak, and Father Sylvan continued to acquiesce to the silence.

Their feet reached the opposite sidewalk. "I appreciate you doing this, Father. I know it was an unexpected request."

"Unexpected but clearly heartfelt." Father Sylvan pointed to the side of the church while he proceeded. "We just need to walk around to the left side of the church, and here we are. The basement door."

Michael looked at the plain metal door. It was tan with a silver doorknob. An old, rusted silver doorknob that Father Sylvan fumbled with for a few seconds before the key did its job. The door, seemingly pained to be moved, creaked when it opened.

"I swear this door is older than I am," Father Sylvan commented. "After you?"

"Thank you." Michael stepped across the threshold onto a small platform. He turned to his left and started to descend into the dark.

"Slow down," Father Sylvan cautioned. "Let me get the, ah, there we go." A light in the stairwell burst to life. It was far brighter than Michael anticipated, and he recoiled before the unanticipated radiance. "Sorry. I should have warned you."

A wave of Michael's hand communicated the acceptance of the apology. Or at least that he had heard. The long, fluorescent light bulbs in the basement hummed and flickered, battling to emit light for perhaps the last time. A total of ten bays stretched along the ceiling and the length of the room. Eight of the ten had both light bulbs working, creating ample visibility.

The room was a wide-open rectangle. No alcoves or nooks were visible, though there was a kitchen and service area across from where they stood. Familiar floor tiles and wood-paneled walls were clear indicators of when the basement was completed. A stack of some forty metal folding chairs on large rolling carts rested against the far wall. Another rack sat much closer to the silent duo. *It's a basement. Just a basement.*

"It's a basement," Michael whispered.

"Yes, it is. Like you said. Bake sales and pasta dinners. Lots of room to set up tables. Kitchen over there. Not ornate, but it gets the job done."

"Yeah. I'm sure. Bake sales and dinners. Maybe a little gathering with cake after Confirmation or First Communion?"

"That too." Father Sylvan looked intently at Michael, who stood in one spot but slowly turned in a circle, occasionally shuffling his feet forward or to the side in his effort to take in the entirety of the room.

When Michael completed his second rotation, he looked at the floor, then at the priest. "That too. Communion and Confirmation." Michael turned his head to look about the room again. When his eyes returned to Father Sylvan's, he was looking through a wall of tears.. "Other things happened in the basements of churches, Father. Sad things. Confusing things."

"Horrific things," Father Sylvan confirmed. He raised a hand to place on Michael's shoulder.

Michael stepped back. His breath was short, and his body was shaken by competing emotions. "I can't—I'm sor—"

"No!" Father Sylvan announced with a force that shook Heaven and made the Devil flee. "No. No. No. There is no sorry from you. Not here. Not now. Apologies. A thousand apologies to you. But no, there will be no sorry from you. I forbid it."

Michael trembled as a fresh round of tears poured. He sobbed, wiping a sleeve across his cheek in an attempt to clear the deluge. "I don't...I can't...." Michael stammered, and he continued to look about the room and back at Father Sylvan.

"May I pray for you?"

"Yes," Michael whispered.

Father Sylvan slowly raised his arm until it split the distance between himself and Michael. "May I?"

"Yes," Michael said, not sure what request he honored but knowing he trusted the man before him. Somehow, in this place, trust was being reborn.

Father Sylvan stepped forward, reaching his fingers toward Michael's face. He ran his thumb through a tear that sought to create a chasm on Michael's cheek. With the tear on his thumb, he traced the sign of the cross on Michael's forehead. "I bless you, Michael Tanner, in the name of the Father, and the Son, and the Holy Spirit. Amen. Heavenly Father, I stand before you this evening with your dear servant, Michael. He stands before you a man of great faith and hope. Of courage and perseverance. He has endured much. I believe him to be weary but unbroken. I ask you, dear Father, to bless Michael with the strength to continue his journey, the wisdom to understand he never walks alone, and the integrity to realize the shame of the wicked is not his shame. He carries too much, so please grant him the grace to release his unnecessary burdens and be free of the anchors that weigh upon him so heavily. I ask you this through the mystery of the Holy Spirit and the compassion of the risen Christ. Amen."

"Amen." Michael forced the word through a sob. He took a few deep breaths while his tears subsided. "May I have the room for a moment, Father?"

"You may," Father Sylvan said, ignoring the accepted protocols for the usage of the basement space when he exited. He reached the top of the stairs and called down, "I will keep the door open for you."

Michael did not acknowledge the final statement. He looked around the room, eyes filling yet again and his nose running. Was there no end to this? Alone, he stood and cried. A thousand emotions swirled in those tears. What pain left him and what anguish remained would be sorted out on the continuing journey of his life. Anger died and forgiveness rose. Forgiving who? Michael ran through names and realized he needed to forgive himself for all the times he felt less of a man. When some foul voice from deep inside condemned him. For the times he was too weak or too angry. For hiding his face or concealing it. For the times he protected others to his own detriment and his inability to break patterns that held him captive. As he wept, one of his visions came to him. He doubled over and bellowed, a scream borne of shame and rage. The haunting question returned. *I am garbage?*

Michael held his head between his hands, allowing cleansing tears to fall while damning those that only carried self-pity and loathing, for they had no place here. A deep breath was drawn as a prelude to bringing one thought to the empty space. "No. No I am not."

Unraveling to his full height, he looked around the room again. No new tears fell, though some remained on his face and had to be wiped away. He did so and exhaled mightily. Breathed deep and exhaled again. A shirt sleeve acted like a tissue when it was run under his nose. Feeling surprisingly composed, Michael walked to the bottom of the stairs and looked up at Father Sylvan standing post at the door. It was time to leave. It was time to get out of the basement.

CHAPTER 24
SIMPLE COURAGE

"Alright," Brian concluded, "let me recap, then I will send us all on our way to unpack and deal with the jet lag."

Sara beamed when she half spoke, half sang her response. "Sounds good. We're in California. We're in California."

"You've been here before."

Sara continued her makeshift, rhythmically challenged song. "But not with this large of an expense account."

Michael laughed. They had been in California for all of four hours, and their different personalities were on display. Brian was in need of a nap, Sara's well of energy was hardly touched, and Michael: he had slept through the night twice in a row. He wondered when he would stop counting.

"An account that can be trimmed," Brian reprimanded, pointing at Sara. In reality, he knew there was nothing to fear, for despite all her talk, Sara was frugal with company money.

"Relax, Dad," Sara said. "I'll be good."

"I know. Anyway, we've arranged a light schedule to get started. Nothing today. Settling in will be enough. Two media appearances in the morning. Early afternoon off, book signing, and two more media obligations in the evening. Our first big presentation is the day after next. I emailed you all the itineraries, but, y'know."

"Well, we do know you like to hear yourself talk to cling to the illusion you're in charge," Michael offered.

Brian sighed. "Okay. I've had enough from both of you. Get out so I can take a nap. Go find your rooms and leave me alone."

"Sure thing, boss." Michael headed for the door.

Sara added, "Get some rest. You're cranky."

Brian growled, an unimpressive growl to be sure, but the effort was there. As they entered the hallway, Sara closed the door just a tad louder than she should have.

"Nice touch," Michael said.

"Thank you. What are you planning on doing?"

"To be honest, I could use a little rest, too. And I need to go over my notes for the presentation. I want to really nail the first one out here. Get things off to a good start."

"You want to work and rest? Boy, did I come out here with the wrong people," Sara teased.

"Actually, I wanted to talk to you about that."

"About you being the wrong people? That's weird, but okay."

Michael laughed. "No, about our downtime. There's a winery about thirty minutes from here. I was thinking, maybe, we could go there tomorrow after my interviews. It has a café. It's on the water. I bet it's beautiful."

"That sounds nice," Sara said with sincerity, "and I agree. We should wait until tomorrow. Brian's not up for that today."

"Oh." Michael debated the wisdom or stupidity of his next words. He opted for stupid. "I was thinking, maybe, just the two of us."

"Oh." Sara nodded her head. "That could be—oh," she repeated, her eyes widening. "Oh! Um, are you asking me on a date?"

"I'm going to go with yes. Not very gracefully, evidently, but yes,

I am. I don't think you have to say much more."

"I," Sara grabbed Michael's arm as he turned away. "I am kinda flattered. And a bit surprised. I'm sorry."

"Well, at least you're kinda flattered. That's actually what I was going for anyway. That and surprised. Two for two. Mission accomplished."

"Michael, I'm just not anywhere near where you would need me to be. I think we are just on different tracks. I like to keep things casual. With you, there would be a bit more on the line."

"I'm not even sure what that means," Michael stated. "It's one lunch. Just a chance to—"

Sara interrupted him. "You know what I mean. Don't play dumb."

"I know. I was just hoping to find some words. But that's foolish. Can't make you feel what you don't feel, now can I? Can I?"

After taking an extended look at Michael, her face became that of a concerned friend. "Are you okay? I know this was—"

"Yeah, I just had to know. I truly enjoy your company and," Michael quickly edited as he spoke, opting for the bare bones reply, "I just had to know."

"I get it," Sara said, her face suddenly turning dark. "Hey, I didn't lead you on, did I? I didn't mean to set you up. I would hate to think I sent you the wrong signal."

"I enjoy your company," Michael moved his hand across his face in an effort to brush Sara's words aside, "which includes your moments of playful energy, contagious laughter, and even the enigmatic brooding. I enjoy you. It was you being you that brought me to this point. Nothing more."

"Nothing?" Sara asked, noticing the slightest hesitation in Michael's words.

"Well, maybe the fact that I'm forty-five and didn't want to let too many more days slip by."

"Fair enough. I'm actually glad you asked. I was kinda wondering lately about—sometimes you, well, you're very nice to me." Sara extended her hand for a formal handshake.

Michael took her hand and turned it so her palm faced the floor. He raised it as if to kiss it but only held it slightly aloft, bowing his head to Sara. She smiled and slowly pulled her hand from Michael's gentle grasp. "You're good people, Sara."

"So are you. We're still going to sell books and kick ass on this tour, right?"

"Oh, hell yeah," Michael responded. "Someone I admire told me I was a superstar. I would hate to let her down."

Sara entered her room. "See you later, superstar."

"Positively." Michael watched the door close and then walked the length of the hallway to reach his room. *At least she didn't run away screaming.* He entered his room and prepared for his day.

Watching his speech, well restrained in mind, let a man never commit
any wrong with his body! Let a man but keep these three roads of
action clear, and he will achieve the way which is taught by the wise.
Through zeal knowledge is gotten, through lack of zeal knowledge is lost;
let a man who knows this double path of gain
and loss thus place himself that knowledge may grow.
-The Buddha, *The Dhammapada*, chapter 20

CHAPTER 25
NEED SHE KNOW?

Michael rubbed his eyes. It was 11:30 p.m. Another successful presentation was in the books. He opted to return to the hotel, despite Brian's prodding. Some other night he would join them for drinks, for there would always be some other night. Tonight he craved solitude. The quiet of his mind and the peace of his soul.

It was already nine days into the two-week California tour. San Diego and Los Angeles had given way to Sacramento and San Francisco. All was running smoothly. Better than expected. The awkward first encounter with Sara after Michael's fumbling attempt to ask her out also occurred. He wished he could laugh at the anxiety he felt regarding any damage he envisioned to their existing friendship. The ground on which he stood was not quite that solid. To be sure, nothing seemed unusual. The two continued to work together effortlessly, both professionally and personally, and their friendship seemed to be enduring Michael's graceless lurching. Even their banter was starting to return.

Still, mental habits created over the years of hiding in and from shadows had made Michael leery of trusting his own perceptions. What if she was merely putting forth a brave front for the sake of maintaining professional cohesion and nothing more? *Maybe I do think too much. Does it even matter?* For eventually, their lives would take them to different destinations and these events would fade from memory.

Perhaps, this was the real issue. He didn't want it to fade away. He didn't wish for Sara to disappear like a mist before the rising sun. Not that he could control how such things would unfold. If they were not meant to be together, this was the inevitable conclusion. Was it this reality that disturbed him so?

Michael shook his head. It could be that simple. One complication remained. One matter he could not shake. Sara had been with him in the flood that became a raging ocean when he opened the Door. Not physically, to be sure, but present. In his thoughts. In his emotions during that desperate meditative struggle. His strength was awakened by affection. What a kindness she gave without knowing it. *She doesn't even know how she changed my life. How could I ever tell her? Now would not be the time for that, but I cannot shake the feeling that she deserves to know the blessing she was to me. I adore her, but she is not mine. She likely never will be. This does not change the gratitude I feel. The debt I can never repay. How do you let someone like that drift from you? I suppose you view it like an act of loving kindness and wish them well. Always wishing them well. Always.*

He hoped he was done thinking about Sara for the night. Smiling, both at his folly and his dreams, at a fool who believed they belonged together. It was likely the false hope of the romantic heart, but the feeling was real on this day. Michael chuckled, the adoration in his heart becoming a source of personal contentment. Arranging the pillows on the headrest so he could both sit and write, he leaned back, sat up, and fidgeted before he struck his pillows in an attempt to induce them to be more comfortable.

The writing session did not last long, just some simple reflections on friendship, loss, and love. How his descent into his personal abyss had strengthened him, despite years of faithless stumbling. How unexpected allies could materialize in times of need, both old friends and new acquaintances that appeared as if written into the story of a life. He was thankful to meet Father Kurt Sylvan. Would this journey even have been possible without their brief interaction? Michael silently promised to send a letter.

Included in his writing was how grateful he was for his current professional success. For his children who brought him such happiness. It was a pleasure, a frightful one at times, but still a pleasure to watch them grow. A few words were dedicated to Carol and Barry, despite his eyelids becoming heavy. His journal found a home on the nightstand, and he yawned deeply. Settling on his side, and because she still drifted about his mind, one last thought: *Goodnight, Sara.* It was barely a statement before he was asleep, peaceful and open to what the next dawn would bring.

Shalom means wholeness, everything fitting together,
nothing missing and nothing broken...shalom for you as an
individual means no fighting with yourself,
no quarreling between the two halves of your divided soul.
To wish someone shalom is to wish him or her the blessing
of wholeness and integrity
-Harold Kushner, from his book *Living a Life That Matters*

The first peace, which is the most important, is that
which comes within the souls of people when they realize their
relationship, their oneness, with the universe and all its powers,
and when they realize that at the center of the universe dwells
Waken-Taka [the Great Spirit], and that
this center is really everywhere,
it is within each of us. This is the real peace, and
the others are but reflections of this.
-Black Elk, *The Sacred Pipe*

CHAPTER 26
A MEDITATION ON HOPE

I stand before you now, here again in the abyss, knowing I am comfortable in your darkness. It holds no horrors for me. Your rough wood and my doorplate. The beautiful arch and the knocker. All here, still, on my Door. Behind you, does the beast still await me? Does he wish to battle more? I believe so. The journey of my life is not complete, and old doubts and fears will rise, giving him strength. But I am strong, too. I confidently walk like a master of the dark, comfortable in the shadows and learning to love the light. I return to you, knowing the beast lingers. My fiercest foe. My dearest friend.

How many times did you crush me? How many times did I flee the shadows to vigorously live half a life? A life that avoided certain experiences, certain joys, because they brought me face-to-face with the shadows? How I feared my weakness. Yet, often times, I would step forward to battle and fail, fall in shame and defeat.

But in the paradox that is the very cornerstone of existence, beaten until my face was rubbed in the mud and filth, it is only by the experience of failure that the half-lived life of divided passion and purpose could be overcome. How many times did I skulk in the dark, defeated and ashamed? How often did I flee back to the stagnant existence that avoids the shadows at all costs? Yet, I always came back to you. The thin strands of hope leading me through a labyrinth of dread into my personal hell. Sometimes all I learned was how to rise up when beaten down. I learned pain can be endured. So I would rise from the ground a little stronger than I was before. Hoping, always hoping, that I would be strong enough to win our next struggle.

Then I fought and fell again. You were always there. Beckoning me. Challenging me. Mocking? But also encouraging? Daring me to become strong? What kind of beast are you? I still do not understand. I do know this: the shadow cannot kill you without your consent. It can only suck the very life from you if you do not struggle with it. Every second fighting the shadow strengthens the soul. Just like an untested dream crumbles before the first sign of resistance, so too can one be said to have no faith until they have walked into the pit of doubt. One does not understand the power of love until the eyes of hate are held by your stare. One who has not tasted betrayal holds loyalty cheap, and grand ideals are only as useful as their ability to keep one afloat in the crushing waves of cynicism and mocking laughter. Hope seeks the furnaces of the deep places to reveal its greatest glory to us.

Your inner world is brought to life when all the distractions, insults, detractors, and paths of the outer world have failed to satisfy. When the half-lived life becomes a prison, one must seek the shadow. To fight. To dance with it. For a reckoning. I wasn't sure I had a soul until I entered my own Tartarus. I did not wish to be divided any longer. I hoped, dared to hope, that the dark path would lead to some salvation. Am I now free to enjoy the outer world without compromising my soul? Can I achieve a beautiful balance that brings authentic peace? What if the beast desired that I live with more harmony, freedom, and passion? Was the beast's rage merely my own?

Is this the final phase of the journey toward the undivided life? Perhaps I must make my shadow feel at home in the light just like I am at home in the dark. If so, we will embark on that great journey at the proper time, whenever that may be. Let me just sit for now. Emboldened by my losses and victories. By love lost and love felt. By the light of enduring hope in the face of despair. Growth is our very nature. It is the unmistakable character of human equality. Like anything else, it may be misused or ignored, but its pull is ever present.

There comes a time for all of us when the shadows of the past must be left behind, and life becomes far more effortless than we thought possible. I do not know where such growth ends. Perhaps with our deaths. Perhaps when we fall into stagnation and lose the drive to explore. All I know is this: I have been blessed to share the gifts of friendship, companionship, peace, grace, and love. I will continue my journey as I hope you continue yours.

CHAPTER 27
KOI PARAGA?

Michael leaned back, attempting to find comfort in the coach section of the airplane which carried him to the Mid-West. His height made that quest difficult but he found a position that required limited contortion. Small victories sometimes make the world go around. In an attempt to distract himself further from his plight Michael produced his copy of *Bruce and Buddha: How Rock and Roll and Ancient Wisdom can be your Guide* and opened to the final pages. He had been reading his own book since arriving in California, new eyes falling on old words.

The Epilogue to Bruce and Buddha: How Rock and Roll and Ancient Wisdom can be your Guide

EPILOGUE
ANSWERING THE CALL

Hello! So glad you're still with me. I truly am. I once read a statistic stating that ninety percent of purchased books are never completed by the purchasers. While not sure how this study was conducted, it inspired me to take stock of my own book collection. After my inventory, I discovered that fifty-five percent of the books in my collection were unread but had been bought with the good intention of reading them. They were quickly pushed down the reading list by five more purchases! And to think, as a college professor, I had time built into my days for research and reading and yet, still that many unloved pages. Therefore, the fact you are here, right now, on the final pages of this book, is a wonderful thing. Good for you.

We've covered a lot of ground, and I will try not to repeat the lessons and stories shared but will focus on some final thoughts before we part company. First, I don't think I have made it to the other shore, nor have I helped you do so. I would, however, contend that you (the reader) and I (the author) have been granted opportunities for reflection. These reflections may have even led to concrete actions, both big and small, in our lives. I know for a fact that I saw myself take some actions because of these words, which I likely would not have undertaken otherwise. These were gratifying occurrences, every one of them. Dear reader, I do hope you enjoyed such benefits. What a compliment that would be.

It is sometimes said that Buddhism is a path or philosophy of life, a sort of blueprint on how to live. Such an understandable thought misses a key element of Buddhism. It is more than a philosophy of life: it was meant to be a rejuvenating path. A path where once you started walking, your life would be renewed. Perhaps bringing an energy to you and your loved ones that you hitherto did not feel. In a day and age of checking off boxes and making lists, it can help us see, know, feel, and experience the deeper meaning behind our daily activities. Maybe that is why the various Buddhas (remember: Buddha is a title meaning "enlightened one." It was never meant to be a singular person) are often depicted as smiling. They simply know something we don't. Maybe that's why Bruce smiles so much.

Once again, I bring you back to Boston and Bruce crying out, "Anyone alive out there?" In that same concert, he mentioned his desire to throw a "rock and roll exorcism" and a "rock and roll bar mitzvah." He became a preacher with a guitar and extolled the audience to find a different path than what they were on. That music, my god, music could be our guide to a better way of life. Let the angels play guitars instead of harps as the sacred waters fall on us and set us free. Free from our petty egos and childish quests for superiority while we seek the betterment of all. May we do so not out of a desire to look politically or morally superior to others, but because the golden cord has been plucked, and we are answering without seeking the adulation of the masses or media. Their attention tends to defile, not revitalize. The revival of our compassion, despite what people may say, is not the goal of many. Crushing opponents and slandering them is what matters most. True compassion seems little more than a fool's dream.

For my last thought, let me leave you with this unique story. When Siddhartha Gautama became the Buddha, he faced a number of challenges from Mara, the great tempter. The last stumbling block Mara put before the young Buddha was the reality of how futile his task was. People would not, Mara insisted, look beyond their selfish desires. People preferred control over compassion, and power always trumped wisdom. Mara stated with confidence that almost no one would listen to the Buddha's words. The few who did would be exhausted by the effort of bringing his lessons to their lives, let alone the world. It was all pointless. Upon pausing to consider the impossibility of his goal, the Buddha smiled. There would be some, few, but some, who would indeed listen. They would hear the call as it continued to be carried forth, perhaps, through the cords struck on a Fender electric guitar purchased at a guitar shop in the heart of New Jersey.

Those few will listen. They will hear. They will find freedom. They will assist others. I do so fervently hope I may have been of service to you just as Bruce and Buddha have gallantly helped me.

Anyone alive out there?

And don't forget: keep fighting the good fight, with all thy might!

THE BOOK WITHIN THE BOOK

Still reading? That's outstanding! Since you're still with me, I am going to allow myself the pleasant thought that you enjoyed the book. Just to be clear, this afterward is being written by James Rourke, author of *Out of the Basement* and not Michael Tanner, the fictional author of *Bruce and Buddha: How Rock and Roll and Ancient Wisdom can be your Guide.* The fact there may be a need to clarify is one of my favorite aspects of this project, and I would like to spend some time with those of you interested in the book within the book.

Various chapters in this book open with epigraphs. This is done for the classic reasons of suggesting a theme and connecting the struggles of one man to the timeless struggle of suffering and over-coming. The first of Buddha's Four Noble Truths is that all of life is suffering. This bleak proclamation is counterbalanced by the other three Noble Truths that present a way to end suffering. Hence the use of Buddha in Michael's fictional work. These epigraphs, how-ever, also serve the purpose of allowing a glimpse into *Bruce and Buddha: How Rock and Roll and Ancient Wisdom can be your Guide.* In chapter four Michael states, "There are great teachers, you see, and I am not one of them." Bruce Springsteen has been one of the great teachers in Michael's life (and mine).

As I wrote, took notes, restructured, and wrote again I came to the conclusion that Michael's book, written to be a guide to his fictional readers, was also acting as Michael's guide. But in order to be an effective guide for Michael *Bruce and Buddha* needed to be grounded in reality. I needed an understanding of the book so it could act as a nonliving but somehow breathing character throughout the story. To that end I penned a few lines of it here and there before settling on the question of what sources Michael would use to make his points.

In an early draft of the book there were a total of eighty-six epi-graphs: forty-eight from books, one from a movie, and thirty-eight song lyrics, with thirty-three of the thirty-eight from Bruce Springsteen's sprawling catalogue. That number was trimmed to sixty-nine in a later draft and currently sits at nineteen. None of these epigraphs are song lyrics. This is due to the decision to offer the "Suggested Listening" list at the start of the book in an attempt to pair certain songs with particular chapters. It also guaranteed inclusion of every song I envisioned from the start be part of this final product. I am exceptionally grateful to my editing partner and professional sounding board, Heather Doughty, for, well, suggest-ing the "Suggested Listening" idea. As with a wine list, it is the pal-ate of the listener that dictates the experience of the pairing. I will not perform a chapter-by-chapter walk-through here, but I would like to offer some insight into my process.

One of the most interesting revelations of the list was how it added credence to a comment made by Michael in Chapter 5. Michael told an audience member, "...the album I used the most was *Darkness on the Edge of Town.*" Sure enough, *Darkness* domi-nates the beginning of the list, with five of the first eleven sugges-tions coming from that album. These entries are the foundation of

Michael's story for, despite the inability to integrate his traumatic experiences effectively, he continues to rise, to fight, and to face the storms of his inner world. Peace is evasive but effort is nonnegotiable. This relentlessness in the face of hardship is a prominent feature of "Racing in the Street," "Badlands," "Darkness on the Edge of Town," and "The Promised Land." Another aspect of these songs is choice— whether it's the character choosing to stay home or head into the night in "Racing in the Street" or the simple use of the word "if" in "The Promised Land"—if the character can head into the storm that threatens to engulf him or ignores the call to battle, acquiescing to defeat before the struggle begins. "Streets of Fire" is, in my eyes, the bleakest of these songs. There is almost no resolve left in the character other than the strength to tell people to stay away from him. It would be the worst possible outcome for Michael and fit the utter defeat experienced in the beating Michael endured in the Chapter 7 nightmare. Moreover, the character's demand for desolate isolation rumbles in Michael and, while he suppresses it well, is revealed most clearly in his early interactions with Melissa Burns.

A true surprise came my way with the compilation of the listening list: the prominence of *Tunnel of Love*. There is a lot of work that goes into merely completing a first draft, let alone the subsequent drafts and re-writes. Keeping track of how often an album was the source for a lyrical epigraph was a nonexistent thought throughout the process. It never even registered as a curiosity. However, once I put the list together the information was revealed. The songs of *Tunnel of Love* generally focus on the fear that accompanies love and the anxiety of relationships in crisis. Only one of the songs, "Tougher than the Rest," is utilized in his pursuit of Sara Torrey. The other four songs use the themes of duplicity, uncertainty, and disappointment to shed light on Michael's inner world, including the moods he tries to shelter people from and the sometimes vicious internal dialogue that undermines his confidence.

I wish to finish this brief discussion with a few thoughts on the ending of *Out of the Basement*. When watching *Bruce on Broadway* on Netflix, Bruce described the opening of "Thunder Road" as an invitation. That invitation is, in some ways, extended again and even simplified in "Tougher than the Rest." Michael having opened the Door and finding the strength for and from a truly cathartic moment with Father Sylvan, extends the invitation to Sara. She does not accept, but this does not leave Michael embittered or resentful, as communicated in "Bobby Jean," our pairing for Chapter 25. For Michael, this song—focused as it is on the power and significance of friendship—is also about the wonder of people who come into our lives with gifts of hope and strength even when they don't realize it. These people may be with us for just one season of our lives but their impact is undeniable, as is their importance.

This brings us to the final chapter. In many ways, the offerings here reveal the other side of the book's opening salvo steeped as it was in *Darkness on the Edge of Town*. "Real World" contains imagery of the personal joy one experiences in moments of pointed personal triumph. There are no grand parades or fireworks, but there is the love, hope, and faith we can carry into our lives. Of course, trials will remain because that seems to be an inexorable characteristic of life. When those demons rise again, "No Surrender" seems like the anthem we need. And if we don't retreat, and if we refuse to surrender, we just might find our highway ends in a sunny place a la "Born to Run."

In Chapter 21, young Michael learned "that music has the power to speak to pain, which is why it also has the power to heal." That's one of the great truths wrapped in this fiction. The greatest example of that, for me, has been the work of Bruce Springsteen. Perhaps his music has served as a guardian angel for you as well.

Be well and remember, keep fighting the good fight with all thy might!

Sincerely,
James Rourke

Writer's Challenge: At the time of writing this, I have been teaching for twenty-four years, so you'll forgive my desire to give a little optional homework.

If you've read this far, you know the power of music. You also know the love of music is best shared. I can't help but wonder what pairings you might think fit best with the chapters, particularly if you liked the book but Springsteen isn't your number one choice in music. Feel free to share your suggested listening list to me at jamesrourkeauthor@gmail.com. Please write "Suggested Listening" in the Subject line. It would be great to hear from you.

Lastly and most important: if you have been moved by Michael's story please consider donating to a national or local organization that supports victims of sexual abuse and strives to end the cycle of violence. Let hope rain down and the healing continue...

CPSIA information can be obtained
at www.ICGtesting.com
Printed in the USA
FSHW021853241120
76118FS